STORYBOOK COLLECTION

DISNEY PRESS
New York

The New Arrival

Every year, the seasons come and go. Icy winter snowflakes melt into beautiful springtime blossoms. The warm summer sun gives way to the brilliant colors of fall. It may seem that these magical changes happen on their own, but in fact, they are all the work of fairies.

Each fairy's life begins as a baby's first laugh. On a cold winter night in London, a baby girl laughed for the first time. The baby's laugh touched a wisp of dandelion fluff. The wisp spun out the window and was carried away by a light breeze.

It floated through the city streets and up toward the Second Star to the Right. The wisp was headed to Never Land!

At it neared the island, the wisp picked up speed.

A fast-flying fairy named Vidia saw it approaching. She created another breeze to help guide it into Pixie Hollow. This was the home of the fairies.

The wisp landed, and the fairies of Pixie Hollow watched as a dust-keeper fairy poured pixie dust over it. Suddenly, a blond fairy appeared! "Hello?" she said as she looked around.

A cloud of shimmering dust approached the new arrival. A beautiful fairy emerged from the cloud. Her wings glowed, and she sparkled with pixie dust. This was Queen Clarion, ruler of all the fairies.

The queen smiled at the little fairy. "Born of laughter, clothed in cheer, happiness has brought you here. Welcome to Pixie Hollow," she said. "Now, let's see about those wings."

Queen Clarion flew behind the new arrival and made two wings sprout from the little fairy's back.

The blond fairy giggled as she flapped her new wings up and down. She could fly! She twirled in the air a few times, then landed with a happy sigh. She thought she was going to like being a fairy.

The queen waved her hands and a circle of toadstools appeared.
Several fairies flew forward, each holding a different glowing
object. The fairies placed their objects on the toadstools and
backed away. "What are these things?" the new arrival asked.

The queen smiled. "They will help you find your talent."

The little fairy was nervous. How would she know which one was meant for her?

She walked up to a flower. But as she reached for it, its glow faded. The same thing happened when she passed by a water droplet and a whirlwind.

As she moved toward a hammer, it began to glow more brightly. Suddenly, the hammer flew into the new arrival's hands.

"Whoa," said a water-talent fairy named Silvermist. "Never seen one glow that much before."

A garden fairy named Rosetta agreed. "Li'l daisy-top might be a very rare talent, indeed."

Queen Clarion laughed. "Come forward, tinker fairies, and welcome the newest member of your talent guild—Tinker Bell."

Two tinker fairies pushed their way to the front of the crowd and introduced themselves to the new arrival. "Haydee hi, haydee ho. I'm Clank," boomed the large one.

"We're pleased as a pile of perfectly polished pots you're here!" said Bobble, a thin fairy with red hair and dewdrop goggles.

The two tinkers took the new fairy by the hand and showed her around Pixie Hollow. There were four different areas, one for each of the seasons: winter, spring, summer, and fall.

Their last stop was Tinkers' Nook, where the tinker fairies worked.

Tinker Bell watched fairies carrying baskets of fruits and acorns. A mouse pulled a cart full of seeds.

"They're taking supplies down to the workshop," Clank explained.

"Right now, fairies of every talent are preparing for my favorite season: springtime!" Bobble exclaimed.

Finally Clank and Bobble showed Tinker Bell to her new home. She changed into a leaf dress, and then hurried back to the workshop.

When Tinker Bell reached the workshop, she looked around in awe.

Clank and Bobble told the new arrival that tinker fairies helped all of the other talents by fixing things and coming up with new inventions.

Just then, Fairy Mary flew in. She was the head of all the tinkers. "Ah, a new charge on whom we can lavish all our tinkering wisdom," she said when she saw Tinker Bell. She inspected the new fairy's hands. "Crack my kettles! So dainty!" Fairy Mary reminded Clank and Bobble to make their deliveries, and then she flew away.

Soon the tinkers were on their way, too. Clank helped a mouse named Cheese pull the cart full of supplies. Suddenly the weeds on the road came to life and chased after the tinkers!

"It's the Sprinting Thistles!" Clank cried.

Crash! The cart full of supplies landed in a flower bed in Springtime Square. Tinker Bell and Bobble tumbled out.

"Are you all right, sugarcane?" Rosetta asked Tink.

Iridessa, a light-talent fairy, helped Tinker Bell up. Bobble stood and pulled the new inventions out of a messy pile.

"Gather 'round, ladies," he said. "We've brought some selections from the spring line of tinker specialties." He handed a rainbow cone to Iridessa.

Silvermist tossed a spray of water into the air. Iridessa flew through the water and created a rainbow. She started to roll the rainbow up and put it in the cone.

"What are you going to do with that?" Tinker Bell asked in amazement.

"I'm going to take it to the mainland," Iridessa said.

"We're going to change winter to spring," Silvermist chimed in.

Tinker Bell couldn't wait to help bring spring to the mainland!

Suddenly, Tink saw a fairy race by in a blur. She told Clank and Bobble that she'd catch up to them and left to chase after the fairy.

"Hi, there," Tinker Bell said. "What's your talent?"

Vidia frowned. "I am a fast-flying fairy," she said. "I make breezes in the summer and blow down leaves in the fall. Fairies of every talent depend on me."

Tinker Bell grinned at her. "Tinkers help fairies of every talent, too!"

But Vidia didn't agree. "It's not like spring depends on *you*," she said.

Tink was furious. "I'll show her," she grumbled as she flew off.

Tinker Bell was so angry that she almost didn't see the shiny object lying on the beach below. The sun glinted off it and shone right into Tink's eyes. She flew down to see what it was.

When she landed on the beach, Tink found all sorts of things. There was a brass bell that jingled when she shook it, a spring that bounced when she pushed on either end, and a silver coin with a grumpy-looking face on it.

Tinker Bell scooped up the objects and rushed off to meet Clank and Bobble.

When she got to the workshop, Tinker Bell showed Clank what she had found. He told her the objects were "lost things."

"Stuff gets lost and washes up on Never Land from time to time. You know, from the mainland," Bobble explained.

As he spoke, Fairy Mary flew into the workshop. When she saw Tinker Bell fiddling with the lost things instead of doing her work, she took them away. Then she reminded the tinkers that the queen would be reviewing their work that evening.

"It's a good time for us tinkers to show what we can do," Clank chimed in.

That gave Tink an idea!

That night, fairies of every talent lined up to show off their hard work.

Tinker Bell pulled up with a cart full of new inventions. "I came up with some fantastic things for tinkers to use when we go to the mainland," she said.

Queen Clarion looked down at Tinker Bell. "Has no one explained?" she asked. "Tinker fairies don't go to the mainland, dear. Those things are done by the nature-talent fairies. Your work is here in Pixie Hollow."

Tinker Bell nodded sadly. Then she gathered her inventions and went back to the workshop. "Being a tinker stinks," she grumbled.

Fairy Mary overheard her. "You are a tinker," she said. "It's who you are. Be proud of it." Then she flew back to her work.

Tinker Bell put her head down on the table and sighed. What's so great about being a tinker? she wondered. Maybe it was the right talent for Fairy Mary, but Tinker Bell didn't think it was the right one for her. She didn't know what she was going to do. She had to find a way to go to the mainland!

A Rare Talent

Tinker Bell was the newest fairy in Pixie Hollow. She was a tinker fairy, but she didn't want to be one. The nature fairies got to help change the seasons on the mainland. Tinker Bell wanted to go there, too. But Queen Clarion, ruler of all the fairies, had told her that a tinker fairy's work was in Pixie Hollow.

Tinker Bell was crushed. Then she had an idea. She would switch her talent!

"I've decided I'm not going to be a tinker fairy anymore," she told her friends as they waited for their daily dose of pixie dust the next morning. "If you could teach me your talents, maybe I could show the queen I can work with nature, too. Then she'd let me go to the mainland!"

"I've never heard of someone switching talents," said Iridessa, a light-talent fairy.

But Tink insisted. "All I'm asking is that you give me a chance," she said.

Silvermist, a water talent, offered to teach Tinker Bell how to place dewdrops on a spiderweb.

Tinker Bell gave it a try. She scooped up a perfect dewdrop from the pond. *Pop!* Water went everywhere.

"Shake it off," Silvermist said. "You can do this!"

Tinker Bell pulled another drop out of the pond. She flew over to the spiderweb and reached out to place the droplet. *Pop!*

She tried and tried, but each time the droplet burst.

Silvermist sighed. "You know, you always struck me as a light fairy kinda gal."

That night, Iridessa showed Tinker Bell how to light fireflies. She used a leaf-bucket to catch the last rays of sunlight. Then she tossed a handful of light into the air. The fireflies flew through the light and came out with their tails lit!

But when Tinker Bell reached into the bucket, the light wouldn't stick to her fingers.

"Argh!" she yelled. "This is impossible!" She threw the bucket on the ground.

Light shot out in every direction! Iridessa and Tink zigged and zagged, trying to avoid the rays, but one of them hit Tink. Her backside began to glow, and the fireflies chased after *her*!

The next day, Tinker Bell was working on a kettle when Fairy Mary flew over.

"I know what you've been up to," she said, shaking her head. "And I had such high hopes for you."

"You'd do well to listen to her," said Bobble, another tinker fairy.

"Why? So I can do this my whole life?" Tink interrupted. "I don't want to be just a stupid tinker!"

As soon as the words were out of her mouth, Tinker Bell knew she shouldn't have said them. Her friends looked at her sadly. "I didn't mean . . . guys . . . I . . . I have to go," she said, and flew out of the workshop.

Tinker Bell felt bad about what she'd said. But she had a new task to keep her busy. Fawn, an animal fairy, was showing her how to teach baby birds to fly.

"Okay, open your wings and flap them up and down," Fawn told a baby bird as she flapped her arms.

The baby bird did what Fawn did, and he started to rise into the air. Fawn asked Tink to help with the last little bird, then she flew away.

Tinker Bell looked at the baby bird. "Hey, little fella," she said. "You wanna do some flap-flap today?" She showed the bird how to flap his wings. But he wouldn't move. He looked scared.

25

Tink sighed. "This is not working," she said.

Just then, she looked up and saw a bird soaring across the sky. "Hey, maybe that guy can help!" She flew toward the bird.

Suddenly, a scout fairy cried, "Hawk!"

The fairies flew for cover. Tinker Bell gasped as the big bird started to chase her. She spotted a knothole in a nearby tree and dove inside.

"Hey!" Vidia said as Tinker Bell crashed into her. "This is *my*

hiding spot! Find your own place to hide!"

Crack! The hawk pushed his beak through the hole and snapped at the fairies.

There was only one way out! The two fairies jumped into a hole and slid down a tunnel. At the bottom, Tink slammed into Vidia and accidentally pushed her out of the tree.

The hawk spotted Vidia and swooped closer.

Suddenly, a berry hit the hawk. The fairies continued to throw berries and rocks until the big bird left.

Tinker Bell hurried over to help Vidia, who was covered in berry bits. But Vidia brushed her off. "I was only trying to help," Tink said.

"Well *stop* trying," Vidia yelled. Then she flew away.

Tinker Bell flew to the beach to think. "At this rate, I should get to the mainland right about . . . *never!*" she grumbled.

She flung a pebble into the bushes. *Clink!* What was that? she wondered.

Beneath the leaves, Tinker Bell found a beautiful box full of metal parts. She immediately set to work. Slowly, the pieces came together. The parts made a music box with a ballerina on top.

Tinker Bell's friends flew over and saw the music box.

"Don't you even realize what you're doing?" Rosetta said. "You're *tinkering!*"

"Don't you like doing this?" Iridessa asked.

"Yeah," Silvermist chimed in. "Who cares about going to the mainland, anyway!"

"I do," Tink replied. She looked at Rosetta. "Aren't you going to teach me how to be a garden fairy?"

Rosetta looked at Tink. "Oh, I think *this* is your talent," she said.

Tinker Bell felt as if her friends were giving up on her. She turned to the only fairy who might help her get to the mainland.

"Vidia, you're my last hope," she said.

Vidia smiled. She told Tink that if she wanted to impress the other fairies, she should capture the Sprinting Thistles.

So Tink and her mouse friend Cheese went off to trap the pesky plants. But when Tink wasn't looking, Vidia set the plants free! The Sprinting Thistles trampled through Springtime Square, ruining all the preparations for spring.

Tinker Bell felt terrible. "I'm sorry," she told Queen Clarion. Then she flew off. She wanted to leave Pixie Hollow forever!

Tinker Bell flew back to the workshop. She looked around at all the tools. She did like to tinker, but she wanted to visit the mainland even more!

Then Tink saw some objects piled in a corner. She went over to look. They were the lost things she'd found on the beach! She thought Fairy Mary had thrown them away.

Suddenly she had an idea. "That's it!" she cried.

Meanwhile, Queen Clarion gathered the fairies together. She told them that there would be no spring that year.

"Wait!" Tink cried, flying up. "I know how we can fix everything!"

She showed everyone the inventions she had made using the lost things. The fairies could use them to redo the work that had been ruined.

"Tinker Bell, are you sure you can do this?" the queen asked.

"Yes," Tink replied proudly. "Because I am a tinker."

Tink told the fairies to bring her all the lost things they could find. Everyone set to work. They didn't have much time.

Early the next morning, Queen Clarion arrived in Springtime Square. All of the supplies were ready!

"You did it, Tinker Bell. You saved spring!" the queen said.

"We all did it," Tink said with a smile.

Suddenly Fairy Mary flew over. She had found the music box Tink fixed.

"You are quite a rare talent indeed," Fairy Mary said. "And I imagine there's someone out there who's missing this. Perhaps a certain tinker has a job to do after all . . . on the mainland."

Tinker Bell couldn't believe it. Her dream was coming true!

The next day, fairies soared through the clouds and across the sea. When they reached the mainland, they fanned out in all directions. They melted the snow and filled the world with color. Tinker Bell had never seen such a magical sight!

Finally it was time for her to return the music box to its owner. Tink flew through the city with the box. When she reached the right house, the box began to glow.

Tinker Bell placed the music box on a windowsill. Then she tapped the glass and hid. She watched as the little girl who lived there found the treasure she'd lost.

Tinker Bell had never been happier. When she got back to Pixie Hollow, she settled into the workshop and began to work on new inventions. From then on, Tink used her rare talent to help all of the fairies with their work. She loved being a tinker after all!

So Long, Pixie Hollow!

The fairies of Pixie Hollow had a lot of work to do. It was their job to bring autumn to the mainland! And that meant gathering a lot of pixie dust. Pixie dust was very important to the

fairies. They could not fly or do their magic without it.

A dust-keeper fairy named Terence was just finishing up his work for the day. "Have you delivered the pixie-dust rations to the scouts yet?" asked Fairy Gary, Terence's boss.

"Finished today's and half of tomorrow's," said Terence.

"Remember, one cup each. No more, no less," warned Fairy Gary.

Suddenly, a beetle buzzer sounded. It was the end of the workday. Terence rushed out to meet his friend Tinker Bell.

Terence found Tink by a stream. She was putting the finishing touches on her new boat. Tinker Bell was a tinker fairy. She loved to fix things and was always tinkering

with spare parts. She proudly showed Terence the *Pixie Dust Express.* She had built it herself!

Terence handed Tink a rubber band. "I thought you could use it for your motor," he explained.

Tink stretched out the piece of rubber. "I think it's going to be perfect," she told Terence, trying not to get tangled in it.

Soon, Tink was ready to test her boat. She launched it onto the water.

"Let 'er rip!" said Terence.

Tink took off. She pulled different levers as she sped up the stream. Out popped wings, skis, and a waterwheel. But the *Pixie Dust Express* was faster than Tink expected. Before she knew it, she had lost control of the boat.

"Oh, no!" Tink cried. Her boat sped onto the shore and crashed into a tree.

Terence rushed over to Tink.

"Are you okay?" he asked as he helped her up.

"Aargh!" Tink cried. She kicked angrily at the sand. "I can't believe the boat broke!" She sat down on the ground, disappointed. Terence sat beside her.

"It just needs a little tinkering," he said. "Now, who do I know who's a good tinkerer?"

Tinker Bell laughed. Terence always knew how to cheer her up. Just then a fairy swooped out of the sky.

"Tinker Bell, Queen Clarion awaits," said the fairy.

Tink wondered why Queen Clarion wanted to see her. Was she in trouble? Tink nervously followed the fairy to Queen Clarion's chamber.

41

Queen Clarion was waiting with Fairy Mary and the Minister of Autumn when Tinker Bell arrived.

"Since time immemorial, fairies have celebrated the end of autumn with a revelry—and this particular autumn coincides with a blue moon," the minister told Tink. "A new scepter must be created to celebrate the occasion."

The minister led her to a room full of scepters. "Every scepter is unique," he said. "Some are the work of animal fairies. Others were made by light fairies or water fairies. This year, it is the turn of the tinker fairies, and Fairy Mary has recommended *you*."

Fairy Mary presented Tink with a sparkling moonstone to place on top of the scepter. On the night of the revelry, the stone would align with the blue moon to create special blue pixie dust. The blue dust kept the Pixie Dust Tree strong.

Tink thanked Queen Clarion, Fairy Mary, and the minister. Then she carefully carried the stone to her workshop.

That night, Tink told Terence about the scepter and the blue pixie dust. Then she showed him the moonstone.

"It's amazing," said Terence. "Maybe I can help you."

"That would be great!" replied Tink.

The next morning, Terence arrived bright and early. He brought Tink all sorts of gadgets he thought she could use for her scepter. He kept the fire going, swept the floor, and even brought Tink her meals. But he also hovered over her. Soon Terence began to get on Tink's nerves.

Finally, Tinker Bell was almost finished with the scepter. She just needed to fix one last piece of it.

"It looks like you need some sort of sharp thingy," said Terence, peering over her shoulder.

He offered to look for something, and Tink gladly let him go. Now she could work in peace. She finished the scepter and placed the moonstone carefully on top. It was perfect!

Just then, Terence returned with a huge, round compass.
"What is this?" Tink asked. "Terence, this is not sharp."

Terence tried to explain that there was a sharp part inside, but Tink pushed the compass out of the way. It rolled right into the scepter! The moonstone popped out, unharmed. But the scepter smashed to pieces.

Tink was furious. "Go away!" she yelled at Terence.

At first, Terence was hurt. Then he got angry. "Fine!" he yelled and stormed out.

When she was alone, Tink kicked the compass with all her might. Its lid popped open— and crushed the moonstone! Tink tried to gather the broken blue bits, but it was no use. The moonstone was ruined!

Tinker Bell tried
to glue the pieces of
the moonstone back
together, but they kept
falling apart. That
night her friends Clank
and Bobble came by.

Tink quickly pushed the pearly blue pieces into a bag. She didn't
want anyone to know about the moonstone.

"We came to see if you wanted to join us for fairy-tale theater,"
said Clank.

"I really don't have time," said Tink, trying to hurry them out.
As they left, Bobble told Tink that Fairy Mary would be at fairy-tale
theater. Maybe Fairy Mary would know where Tinker Bell could
find another moonstone.

"Clank, Bobble, wait for me!" she called.

At the fairy-tale glen, Tinker Bell hurried over to Fairy Mary.

"I was thinking," said Tink nervously, "if using one moonstone creates a little blue pixie dust, using two would create even more. Is there another moonstone?"

Fairy Mary laughed. "That moonstone is the only one found in the last hundred years."

Tinker Bell was in even more trouble than she thought! Just then the lights dimmed. A fairy named Lyria came onstage.

With a swirl of pixie dust, Lyria began to tell a story about a mirror that had the power to grant one wish. According to legend, the mirror had been stolen by pirates. But their ship had run aground on a mysterious island, and the mirror was lost forever.

Lyria told the fairies about the three signs that would lead to the lost island: a stone arch, an old troll bridge, and an abandoned ship that sunk but never sank.

Tinker Bell's eyes grew wide. She had to find that mirror!

Tinker Bell rushed home and began to draw a map to the lost island. She checked the compass Terence had left. Then she gathered food, clothing, and other supplies.

How am I going to carry all this? Tink wondered. She looked into her bag of pixie dust. She didn't have enough to make a long journey.

The next morning, Tinker Bell went to ask Fairy Gary for more pixie dust.

"You know the rules," he said. "You already got your ration."

But Tink was determined. She asked her friends Iridessa, Rosetta, and Silvermist if they could lend her some dust, but they had none to spare. Finally, Tink asked Terence.

"Why do you need more dust?" he asked.

Tink grew angry. "A true friend wouldn't ask!" she yelled.

"A true friend wouldn't ask me to break the rules!" Terence yelled back.

"Well, then, I guess we're not true friends," Tink said. She stormed off.

On her way home, Tink kicked angrily at a cluster of cotton balls. A sprinkle of pixie dust fell out of her bag and onto the cotton, which began to float.

Suddenly, Tink had an idea. She collected all the cotton balls she could carry and a large, hollow gourd. Then she got to work.

Tink drilled. She sawed. She nailed. When she was done, she had built a balloon to bring her and all of her supplies to the lost island.

As the sun began to go down, Tink put the compass and her supplies in the balloon. She very carefully placed the moonstone pieces in a bag and tied it around her waist. Then she sprinkled some pixie dust on top of the cotton-ball balloon. The whole thing began to float!

Tink was thrilled. She and her balloon rose higher and higher into the sky.

"So long, Pixie Hollow!" she called. "I'll be back soon!"

A Glowing Team

Tinker Bell was on her way to a lost island. She had been asked by the Minister of Autumn to create a scepter for the autumn revelry using a rare blue moonstone. The stone would align with the moon and supply the fairies with special blue pixie dust. But Tink had broken the moonstone. Now, she was searching for the legendary Mirror of Incanta, which would grant her one wish. It was her only hope for replacing the moonstone!

As night fell, Tink grew hungry. She opened a bag of food, but it was empty. She opened another bag. Inside was a very cute little firefly—with a very full stomach. The firefly had eaten all her food!

"Out! Shoo!" Tink yelled at the little firefly.

"I'm on a very important mission," she said. "I have two days to find the magic mirror and wish the moonstone back."

Tink pulled out her map. But it was too dark outside. She couldn't read it.

Suddenly a gentle light lit up the map. It was the firefly!

"Oh, all right," Tink told him. "You can stay. I'm Tinker Bell. What's your name?"

The firefly glowed even more brightly.

"Blinky? Flicker?" Tinker Bell guessed. Then she got it. "Blaze!"

As the balloon flew through the night sky, Tink and Blaze kept watch for the lost island. Suddenly the balloon floated into a thick fog. They could no longer see where they were going. The two friends settled down and soon dozed off.

The next morning, they woke up to a loud crash. The balloon had flown into a tree and gotten stuck on a branch.

"This must be the lost island," Tink said. "There it is! The stone arch from the story!" Tinker Bell asked Blaze to stay and watch the balloon. Then she flew off to investigate.

Tink could barely contain her excitement as she hurried toward the arch. But when she got closer, she realized it was made of two trees, not of stone. It was the wrong arch!

Just then, Blaze flew over. The anchor had come loose, and the balloon was floating away! He tried to warn Tink, but she was too busy thinking about the arch to listen. By the time she realized what had happened, the balloon was gone.

Tink was lost. She was sad. And she was hungry.

Blaze wanted to help. He gave a distress call, and a group of bugs appeared. Bees brought Tink honey to eat and pill bugs gave her  water. Soon, Tinker Bell felt much better.

"Have you seen a stone arch around here?" Tink asked.

The bugs helped Tinker Bell to her feet and led her to a clearing in the forest. A big stone arch lay just across the valley.

"Thank you so much," Tink said. "It's great to have friends that'll help you out, huh?" she said to Blaze.

Suddenly, Tink felt a wave of sadness. She missed her friend Terence. The last time she saw him, they'd fought and she'd stormed off.

Back in Pixie Hollow, Terence missed Tink, too. He decided to go apologize to her. But when he knocked on her door, there was no answer.

"Tink, it's me," Terence called. "There's something I need to tell you. Tink?"

Terence opened the door and peered into Tink's room. "Anyone home?" he asked. He took a few steps and felt something crunch under his feet.

"The moonstone!" he gasped. Terence looked around and found Tink's checklist and balloon plans. He didn't know where his friend was, but it looked like she needed help.

Tink and
Blaze passed
through the stone
arch and came
to an old troll
bridge. They had
found the second
clue! But the
trolls wouldn't let
them pass.

"Beat it before we grind your bones to make our bed," said the smaller troll.

"Make our 'bread,' not 'bed,'" said the taller troll.

The trolls began to argue back and forth.

They were so distracted by their fight that they didn't notice Tink and Blaze tiptoe past them and over the bridge.

Blaze flew across the island, and Tinker Bell walked beside him. She was out of pixie dust and couldn't fly. Soon they reached a long stretch of beach. Tink spotted a wrecked pirate ship. She felt a jolt of excitement. This was the place!

"The ship that sunk but never sank," she said. "Blaze, this is it! We've got to find that mirror and fix the moonstone. Let's go!"

Tink and Blaze took off toward the ship.

Inside, the ship was dark and damp. It creaked with every step they took. Shadows flickered all around the frightened pair.

Tink felt something brush past her. "Who's that? Who's there?" she called. But there was no response.

"Look, Blaze," whispered Tink. She pointed to a satchel sitting on top of an old table. The mirror had to be in it!

Tinker Bell jumped up and tried to grab the satchel, but it was too high for her. Then she remembered a sharp, pointy needle she had brought with her. She threw the pointy needle at the satchel. *RIIIP!* The needle caught the bag's fabric and tore it wide open. Gold and jewels and other pieces of lost fairy treasure poured out onto the floor.

Tink jumped on the pile and began to search for the mirror. "It's got to be in here somewhere," she told Blaze. "Help me look."

Suddenly, Blaze's glow reflected off a shiny object in the pile. It was the mirror! Tink reached in and pulled it out.

Tink looked into the mirror. "Only one shot at this," she said, trying to concentrate.

But just as Tinker Bell was about to make her wish, Blaze started buzzing in her ear.

"Blaze, I wish you'd be quiet for one minute!" yelled Tink.

Blaze's buzzing stopped.

Tinker Bell gasped. "No, that one didn't count!" she shouted. "That wasn't my wish! Blaze, look what you've done!"

Blaze nuzzled up to Tink and tried to apologize. Tinker Bell looked at her silent friend and began to cry.

"I'm sorry, Blaze. It's not your fault," she admitted. "It's mine. All mine."

"I wish Terence were here," said Tink sadly. "I wish we were still friends."

Suddenly, Terence's face appeared in the mirror. "I *am* here," he said.

Tink glanced over her shoulder. Terence was right behind her!

"Terence!" cried Tinker Bell. She gave her friend a big hug. "I'm so sorry. But how did you . . . ?"

"I flew all night and all day," Terence explained. "Just when I was going to run out of dust, I stumbled into that flying machine of yours. It got me the rest of the way here. But why didn't you tell me about the moonstone?"

"I didn't think I needed any help," Tink said. "I was wrong."

Just then, a pack of giant rats jumped out of the shadows. They chased after the fairies!

Terence grabbed Tink and swung her across the room on a curtain. They spotted an opening in the floor and jumped down.

"Terence, buy me some time," called Tink. She threw him the needle and ran behind some debris. Terence fought off the rats while Tink used Blaze's light to make the shadow of a terrifying monster appear on the wall.

Tinker Bell's plan worked! The rats scurried away in fear.

"Let's go!" said Terence.

Tink, Terence, and Blaze made it safely back to the balloon. With a dash of pixie dust, they set sail.

"What's going to happen when we get back?" asked Tinker Bell.

"I don't know if it will help," replied Terence, "but I brought this." He took out Tink's shattered scepter.

Tinker Bell took a piece of moonstone out of her pouch. She had an idea.

"I can't do this without you," she told him. "Would you help me?"

Tink and Terence worked through the night to fix the broken scepter. Behind them, the blue moon rose higher and higher in the sky.

Back in Pixie Hollow, the autumn revelry had begun. Queen Clarion and the Minister of Autumn were onstage. Fairy Gary was ready to collect the blue pixie dust. But Tinker Bell was nowhere to be found.

"This is a disaster!" cried Fairy Mary.

Suddenly, Tink and Terence arrived in the balloon. Tinker Bell climbed out and bowed to the queen.

"Where is the autumn scepter?" asked Queen Clarion.

"There were . . . complications," said Tink. "But it's ready now." Terence handed her the scepter, wrapped in a leaf.

"Fairies of Pixie Hollow," said Tinker Bell. "I present the autumn scepter." She pulled off the leaf to reveal a scepter made of broken bits of metal, pieces of moonstone, and the magic mirror.

"Please work," whispered Tink.

As the moon's rays touched the scepter, moonbeams reflected everywhere. A shower of blue pixie dust began to fall on the crowd.

"I've never seen this much blue pixie dust before!" cried the minister. The other fairies watched in delight as pixie dust swirled around them.

Queen Clarion stepped forward. "Tonight is our finest revelry ever," she announced. "Thanks to one very special fairy—Tinker Bell."

Tink pointed to Terence. "And her friend Terence," added the queen.

Blaze flew between Tink and Terence, buzzing happily. "And her new friend . . ." added Queen Clarion.

"Blaze," said Tink.

The crowd of fairies clapped and cheered for the best autumn revelry ever—and the three friends who had made it possible.

A Magical Friend

Tinker Bell and her friends soared through the sky. They were on their way to bring summer to the mainland.

Summer was the fairies' busiest time of year. They would have to stay on the mainland for a few months to get all their work done.

Tinker Bell's friend Terence, a dust-keeper, flew up next to her on a white dove. "Hey, Tink," he said. "Ready for your first summer on the mainland?"

"Absolutely!" Tink exclaimed. She had never been so excited.

"Well, what are we waiting for? Race you down!" Terence swooped off on the dove.

The nature fairies got to work right away. Vidia, a fast-flying fairy, stirred up summer breezes. Silvermist, a water fairy, met new pollywogs. Rosetta, a garden fairy, sang to the flowers and opened blooms. And Iridessa, a light fairy, guided sunbeams to bright yellow sunflowers.

Tink and Terence landed in a meadow. He led her over to the base of an old oak tree. There, beneath the cluster of leaves, was a camp bustling with fairies. Everyone was very busy preparing for the new season.

Tinker Bell couldn't wait to get to work herself! At the moment, though, there was nothing to fix. Everything seemed to be working.

"You'll find something to fix," Terence reassured her.

Tink knew he was right. While she waited, she decided to go look for some lost things. But before she could leave camp, Vidia flew into her path.

"Hold on, Little Miss Spare Parts," Vidia said. "You're not going near the *human* house, are you?"

Tink's eyes grew wide. "There's a human house?"

"Tink knows we have to steer clear of the humans or we won't be able to get our work done," Iridessa said. "*Right*, Tink?"

Suddenly, a loud noise echoed through the camp, startling the fairies.

Fawn, an animal talent, splattered paint on the wing of a butterfly she'd been decorating. "Oh!" she cried as it fluttered away.

The other fairies quickly hid under leaves.

One fairy, however, was curious about the noise. Tinker Bell flew high above the oak tree and spotted a car driving down a long, winding road. She chased after the car. She had to get a closer look!

"Tinker Bell!" Vidia called out. But Tink was already gone. Vidia had no choice but to follow.

The two fairies followed the car to a house in the country.

A little girl named Lizzy got out with her father, Dr. Griffiths, and their cat, Mr. Twitches.

"Thank goodness we're here, Father!" Lizzy said. "Look at the creek and the woods and the meadow! I wish it was summer all year long!"

When the humans had gone inside, Tinker Bell flew up to the car for a closer look. "Vidia, this is amazing!" she cried.

Tink zipped into the engine to see how all the parts worked.

"Tinker Bell, you shouldn't be this close to the human house," Vidia scolded. "Will you stop flitting around in there?"

But Tink wasn't listening. She had found an interesting lever. "Let me know if this does anything," she called to Vidia as she pulled the lever over and over.

Outside the car, Vidia was hit with several cold blasts of water.

Just then, Lizzy and her father came back outside. Tink and Vidia rushed under the car to hide.

"Father, look!" Lizzy said.

The fairies watched as a butterfly with paint splattered across one wing landed on Lizzy's finger. It was the one Fawn had been decorating!

"The wings have two entirely different patterns," Dr. Griffiths said. He knelt beside Lizzy for a closer look. "That's nearly impossible!"

"Well, I guess that's just the way the fairies decided to paint it," Lizzy said with a smile.

"Lizzy," Dr. Griffiths said. "Fairies do not paint butterfly wings because, as you know, *fairies* are not real."

Dr. Griffiths was a scientist. He took out his field journal, which was filled with facts, and began to sketch the butterfly.

Lizzy pulled a fairy house she'd built out of the car. She wanted her father to take her to the meadow, but he was too busy. Lizzy skipped off on her own while Dr. Griffiths followed the butterfly.

When the coast was clear, Tinker Bell and Vidia came out from under the car. Vidia couldn't fly with wet wings, so the fairies began to walk back to their camp.

As they passed through the meadow, Tink spotted a trail of buttons. She started to stack them in her arms.

Suddenly, Vidia stopped in her tracks. The buttons led right to Lizzy's fairy house!

Tinker Bell wanted to explore, but Vidia didn't. "Let's go!" they said at the same time.

"Tinker Bell, we're not supposed to go near human houses!" Vidia said.

But Tink was already walking inside.

Vidia decided to teach Tinker Bell a lesson. With a gust of wind, she blew the door shut. "Not so safe now, is it?" she called.

Suddenly, Vidia heard someone coming. She tugged on the door, but it wouldn't budge. Tinker Bell was trapped inside!

Vidia watched in horror as Lizzy peered into the house. The little girl was delighted to see a real fairy. Then she picked up the house and took it home.

Vidia followed Lizzy back to her house. She watched as the little girl put Tinker Bell in a birdcage to keep her safe from the cat. Vidia had to save Tink!

The fast-flying fairy raced back to camp. "Tinker Bell's been captured by humans!" she yelled when she arrived.

The fairies gathered around. The needed a plan to rescue their friend. Thunder rumbled and storm clouds gathered. Suddenly it started to rain.

"We can't fly in the rain," Fawn pointed out.

But Clank and Bobble, two tinker fairies, had an idea. They would build a boat.

Back at Lizzy's house, the little girl let Tink out of the birdcage. "I'm not going to hurt you," she said.

Lizzy showed Tinker Bell her fairy drawings. Tink

realized that the girl loved fairies. But she had her facts all wrong!

Just then Dr. Griffiths came into the room. Tink hid and listened as Lizzy's father gave her a journal. He wanted her to use it for scientific research.

When Dr. Griffiths left, Lizzy asked Tinker Bell to help her fill the journal with facts about fairies. Tink couldn't fly back to camp because of the rain, so she agreed to help the little girl.

Meanwhile, Tinker Bell's friends had finished building their boat. They set off down a flooded path through the meadow.

The wind and rain made the trip dangerous. The fairies raced along the rapids, and were soon headed for a waterfall!

Thinking quickly, Silvermist dipped her fingers in the water. She made the water level rise so the drop over the falls wouldn't be so steep. The boat sailed over the roaring water and crashed into the grass on the shore. Everyone was all right, but the boat was badly damaged.

"Looks like we're walking from here," Vidia said.

At the Griffithses'
house, Tinker Bell and
Lizzy finished working
on the journal.

The rain had
stopped and Tink was
preparing to head
back to camp. As
she stepped up to the
window, she heard

Lizzy trying to show her father the journal.

"Father, look," Lizzy said. She held out the journal.

"I don't have time!" Dr. Griffiths said. "I have to find some
way to deal with these leaks before they destroy my work."

Lizzy sadly turned and went back to her room.

Tinker Bell flew up there to meet her.

Lizzy sat on her bed. Tears fell onto the pages of her journal. Her father never seemed to have any time for her.

Suddenly, a small shadow appeared over the page.

"Tinker Bell!" Lizzy exclaimed. "You came back. Oh, Tinker Bell, Father has no time for the field journal."

Tink smiled. She wiped a tear from Lizzy's cheek. "I think I can fix that," she jingled.

Tinker Bell was the best tinker fairy in all of Pixie Hollow. She knew she could help Lizzy. She just had to figure out how. . . .

Faith, Trust, and
Pixie Dust!

Tinker Bell's friends knew she was a curious fairy. She liked to try new things and was fascinated by shiny machines with parts that moved. Her curiosity made her a really good tinker fairy. But sometimes, it got her into trouble.

Now, her friends were on their way to rescue her from a little girl named Lizzy. Tink had been captured when she'd wandered into a fairy house Lizzy had made. Vidia, a fast-flying fairy, had seen it all and was leading a rescue party to Lizzy's house.

The fairies had been sailing in a boat because they couldn't fly in the rain. Then the boat crashed, and they had started walking instead.

Vidia was helping the other fairies across a muddy road when she got stuck. She tried to use her wings to lift herself up, but they were still soaked. "I can't get myself out of here!" Vidia grumbled.

The fairies surrounded her and pulled as hard as they could.

Suddenly, a beam of light shone on the fairies. A car was coming right toward them!

Rosetta, a garden fairy, tugged harder on Vidia. "Pull! Pull!" she said.

Thinking quickly, Iridessa, a light-talent fairy, stuck her hand into the beam of light. She bent it back toward the driver. The car skidded to a stop. The door opened, and the driver stepped out. "Hello?" he called.

Fawn, an animal talent, noticed that the driver's shoelace

was untied. "Grab this! Hurry!" she said.

The fairies grabbed the shoelace. As the driver turned to get back into his car, they were pulled out of the mud!

Meanwhile, Tinker Bell and Lizzy had become good friends. Lizzy's father, Dr. Griffiths, was busy with his work. He'd also been trying to fix a leaky ceiling. That didn't leave him much time for Lizzy.

Tinker Bell had promised the little girl that she would help.

She flew into the attic, and with a little tinkering, she fixed the leaks!

On her way back to Lizzy's room, Tink spotted a butterfly trapped in a jar. She wanted to help it, too, so she opened the jar and set it free.

A few hours later, Dr. Griffiths noticed that the leaks had stopped. Then he saw that the butterfly was no longer in its jar. He'd captured it for his research and was planning on taking it to the museum.

He showed Lizzy the empty jar. "The butterfly is gone," he said. "Did you release it?"

Lizzy was as surprised as her father. "No . . ." she replied.

"Well, I didn't do it," he said. "And since there is no one else in the house, there's only one logical explanation. It must have been you."

"I didn't do it, Father," Lizzy said.

But Dr. Griffiths didn't believe his daughter. "I'm very disappointed in you," he said, and sent Lizzy to her room.

Tinker Bell felt terrible! She had wanted to fix things so Lizzy could spend more time with her father. She hadn't meant to make the situation worse!

Outside, Tinker Bell's friends were nearing the house. They missed Tink and hoped she was safe.

Suddenly, Vidia stopped everyone. "Tinker Bell getting trapped is my fault," she blurted out. She told the other fairies that she had tried to teach Tink a lesson by shutting her in the fairy house.

"Oh, honey," Rosetta said, "this is not your fault. Tink can get

into plenty of trouble all by herself."

Vidia was shocked. "I don't know what to say."

Rosetta held out her hand. "How about faith . . ."

"Trust," Iridessa chimed in.

Vidia clasped hands with the others. "And pixie dust!"

Back in Lizzy's room, Tinker Bell was trying to cheer up her new friend.

"I wish I were a fairy . . . just like you," Lizzy said.

That gave Tink an idea! She motioned for Lizzy to close her eyes. Then, Tink sprinkled her with pixie dust.

Lizzy's feet started to lift off the floor. She grabbed on to the bedpost.

Tink gave her friend a reassuring smile. She showed the girl how to move her arms and legs.

"I'm flying!" Lizzy exclaimed. "Look at me! I'm a fairy!"

Tink and Lizzy were having a great time. But the sound of Lizzy's laughter brought Dr. Griffiths to the room.

Lizzy told her father that a fairy had taught her to fly. Dr. Griffiths was upset. He didn't want his daughter to waste her time on make-believe.

Tink wanted to help, so she flew right up to Lizzy's father.

Dr. Griffiths gasped. Then he grabbed a jar and lowered it toward Tinker Bell.

"Tink! Watch out!" Vidia called. She'd arrived just in time! She zoomed over and knocked Tink out of the way. The jar came down over her instead!

Dr. Griffiths ran out of the room with Vidia trapped in the jar. Lizzy tried to stop him, but he wouldn't listen. The fairy was the discovery of the century! He couldn't wait to show her off at the museum.

Tinker Bell knew she had to save Vidia. But she couldn't do it alone. She was going to need some help!

Just then, the rest of the rescue party arrived. They'd been distracting Lizzy's cat, Mr. Twitches, so Vidia could get to Tink.

Tinker Bell told the fairies where Dr. Griffiths was taking Vidia. But the rain had started again. The fairies couldn't fly to the museum.

Then Tinker Bell had an idea. Lizzy could fly!

The fairies helped Lizzy put on a raincoat and hat. "I'm scared, Tinker Bell," the little girl said.

Tink gave her new friend an encouraging look. She believed in Lizzy. And Lizzy believed in Tink!

"Okay, I'll be brave," the girl said.

The fairies showered Lizzy with pixie dust. She started to lift off the floor, and Tink slipped into her collar. "All aboard!" Tinker Bell said.

The other fairies climbed into Lizzy's coat pockets.

Lizzy rose higher and higher. She flew through the kitchen door and up, up, up into the sky.

"I'm doing it!" she cried as she soared through the clouds. "I'm flying!"

Lizzy and the fairies were on their way. They had to stop Dr. Griffiths!

Soon, the group spotted city lights twinkling below. Lizzy dipped under the clouds. She searched the streets for her father's car.

"There he is!" she said, pointing.

Tinker Bell took off after the car. She flew up beside it and saw Vidia inside in the jar.

Vidia was surprised to see her. "Tink!" she called.

Tinker Bell nodded. Then she dove beneath the car.

"Tinker Bell, no!" Vidia cried. But Tink was already out of sight.

Under the car, Tink studied the engine. It was full of dangerous moving parts. She tried to stay out of their way as she pulled on pipes and wires.

The engine began to spark and sputter. Finally, the car came to a stop.

Dr. Griffiths banged on the steering wheel. "No, no, no!" he yelled. He was so close to the museum! He jumped out of the car with the jar and began to run.

Lizzy caught up to her father on the steps of the museum. "Father!" she called.

Dr. Griffiths turned. He gasped when he saw Lizzy flying toward him. "You're . . . flying," he said. "I . . . I don't understand."

Tinker Bell and the other fairies fluttered around Lizzy. "You don't have to understand," Lizzy said. "You just have to believe."

Dr. Griffiths couldn't take his eyes off the fairies. "I do believe," he said slowly. "Oh, Lizzy, I'll never doubt you again!" He opened his arms and Lizzy rushed into them.

Then, Dr. Griffiths handed the jar to his daughter. She unscrewed the lid and smiled as Vidia flew out.

Tinker Bell wrapped Vidia in a hug as the other fairies surrounded them. The fairies flew over Lizzy and her father and sprinkled them with pixie dust.

"Why, I'm flying!" Dr. Griffiths said. Lizzy giggled.

Together, they rose over the city streets and flew home.

The next day, the fairies joined Lizzy and her father for a tea party in the meadow. When they had finished their tea and snacks, everyone sat back and listened as Dr. Griffiths read from Lizzy's fairy journal.

Tinker Bell's friend Terence flew up beside her. "Well, Tink, you found something to fix after all!"

Tink looked at Lizzy and her father. "I guess I did," she said with a smile.

The Unlucky Ladybug

"Silvermist!" Iris, a garden-talent fairy, called out as she rushed up with an armful of chrysanthe-poppies. "Thanks for waiting!"

Silvermist, a water talent, sat up in her canoe. The fairies were having a picnic on an island not far from Pixie Hollow. Silvermist had promised Iris she would bring the flowers there for her.

Iris carefully put the chrysanthe-poppies in the canoe.

"See you there!" Silvermist said, paddling off.

"Moving a bit slowly today, sweetheart?" asked Vidia, landing lightly on the end of the canoe.

"Hi, Vidia. Are you going to the picnic?" Silvermist asked.

Vidia laughed. "Goodness, no."

"How are my flowers?" Iris shouted from the water's edge.

"Flowers? Is that what those weeds are?" Vidia asked, leaning over to look.

Suddenly the canoe tipped . . . and Vidia fell backward into the water!

Vidia waved her arms in alarm. A crowd of fairies flew over and helped her up.

The canoe bumped against the shore. Silvermist climbed out and hurried to Vidia, who sat dripping on the beach. "Are you all right?"

"I'm f-f-fine," Vidia snapped. "Next time don't rock the boat." She shook her long, wet ponytail and stormed off.

Silvermist felt terrible about what had happened. But she was still enjoying the picnic.

After lunch, Beck, an animal-talent fairy, suggested they play spots and dots. Beck gathered dozens of ladybugs that wanted to play. The ladybugs had ten seconds to hide. Then the fairies had to find as many of them as possible and count their dots. The fairy with the highest score won.

When it was time to search for the ladybugs, Silvermist checked every hiding place she could think of. She found one ladybug in a bush. Another was hiding in a nest. Then she spotted an unusual-looking ladybug. It was milky white, and its dots were white, too.

To her surprise, the white ladybug hopped on her head.

"Hey!" Silvermist called out to the other fairies. "Do I get extra points if a ladybug finds *me*?"

Silvermist's friends gathered around her.

"White ladybugs bring bad luck!" Iris gasped.

A hush fell over the picnic. Fairies were superstitious creatures. They believed in wishes, charms, and luck—both good and bad.

Silvermist shook her head, trying to get the ladybug to fly away. But it wouldn't.

"Here, let us help." Beck and Fawn, another animal-talent fairy, lifted the ladybug and carried it to a tree.

"Let's play fairy tag," Fira, a light talent, suggested. She looked around at the fairies. Finally she tapped Silvermist. "You're it!" she said.

Silvermist waited while her friends scattered. Then she flew after Beck.

"Yoo-hoo, what about me?" Fawn called.

Silvermist turned to chase Fawn—and crashed into a tree trunk.

"Ouch!" she cried, fluttering to the ground.

"Well, that was a little strange," Silvermist said.

"Strange? It's terrible! You're cursed, Silvermist!" Iris said, backing away.

Fira landed beside Silvermist. "Goodness! What happened?"

"It was just an accident," Silvermist said.

"I don't think so," said Vidia, who was stuck on the island until her wings dried. "A fairy needs to be pretty unlucky to fly into a tree."

Everyone stared at Silvermist. She couldn't believe it. Were they really scared of a harmless ladybug?

"There's no such thing as bad luck," she told the other fairies. "I'm not going to pay attention to this crazy superstition and neither should you."

"Any fairy could have a little flying accident," Silvermist told herself later. Still, she knew her friends thought she had bad luck and that she was cursed.

But I don't believe it, Silvermist thought as she flew back to the Home Tree. Maybe she could help the cooking fairies get ready for dinner.

"Hi, Dulcie," she said, flying into the kitchen. "Anything I can do?"

Dulcie quickly shook her head. "We're all set. You don't even have to come inside," she said.

"Just let me fill the water pitchers," Silvermist said, landing at the water pump. She caught the flowing water and sent it streaming over Dulcie's head into a pitcher.

At that moment, Vidia swept into the kitchen. "I was just flying past and saw you here, Silvermist. Any more accidents?"

"Nope." Silvermist shot another stream into the pitcher. "Not one." But when she turned, her wing brushed against a pitcher. The pitcher tipped over and fell against another pitcher. Silvermist tried to catch them, but she wasn't fast enough.

Water splashed onto the honey buns and into the walnut soup. Fairies rushed around the room with moss mops and towels.

"Hmmm," Vidia said smugly. "Looks like dinner might be late tonight."

During dessert, Silvermist reached for the sugar bowl and knocked over the pepper. "Oops!"

"Oh!" Iris moaned. "That's bad luck, too!"

"Quick! Toss some over your left shoulder!" Fira urged.

Silvermist threw a handful of pepper over her shoulder . . . right into the face of a serving talent! He sneezed and the platter of pudding he was carrying crashed to the floor.

Maybe I *do* have bad luck, Silvermist thought sadly as the fairies and sparrow men filed quietly out of the Tea Room. Maybe the curse is real!

The next morning, Silvermist felt better. She flung open her window to let in the fresh air.

Chirp! A cricket hopped onto a branch outside her window and began to sing.

Silvermist smiled. If she were really unlucky, would a cricket sing her a special song?

But when she flew into the courtyard, she found out there had been a songbird concert—and that she had missed it.

Silvermist felt tears coming on. She was the kind of fairy who flew into trees. And tipped over water pitchers. And missed songbirds. No doubt about it—Silvermist was unlucky.

Word spread quickly that Silvermist had missed the concert.

"I told you! She's cursed!" Iris said, fluttering from fairy to fairy.

Rani called the worried fairies to attention. "I have an announcement. There will be a waterball tournament tomorrow. All water talents are invited to show their skills!"

"I'm sure Silvermist won't be taking part due to a severe case of bad luck," Vidia said.

Silvermist frowned. "Vidia is mistaken," she said, smiling at Rani. "I will be there."

The water talents cheered. Silvermist knew she had done the right thing. But still, she was worried.

"I just know something's going to go wrong," she told Fira as they left the courtyard.

"Let's visit the library," Fira suggested. "It might give us an idea."

The two fairies found lots of books on superstition. Silvermist learned that the curse of the white ladybug was a very powerful one. But she also found out she could undo the curse with a good-luck charm.

The fairies made a list of things they could do to bring good luck.

"Find a five-leaf clover," Silvermist said. But that would take too long. "What about 'collect a swan feather'?"

"Let's try it!" Fira said.

The fairies flew to Crescent Lake. "Look!" Silvermist cried. "Two swans!" The swans floated past a nest built on the bank.

The fairies flew to the nest. "No feathers," Silvermist said.

"That's okay." Fira flapped her wings. "We'll go after them. They're bound to lose one feather!"

Silvermist started to follow Fira, but her dress snagged on a twig. Suddenly she heard a flutter.

"Fira?" she called.

But it wasn't Fira. It was an angry black swan!

Silvermist was able to tear her dress free, and she and Fira flew safely back to Pixie Hollow. But I still don't have a good-luck charm, she thought worriedly.

The next day, Silvermist arrived bright and early at the contest field. Queen Clarion sat on a colorful mat near the targets. Fairies and sparrow men milled about, talking and laughing.

"Water talents, take your places behind the line," the queen announced. "You each have five tries to hit the target."

Each of the water talents took a turn until only Silvermist was left. She scooped up the water and made her throw.

The waterball soared through the air toward the target . . . and hit Queen Clarion in the face!

Silvermist could barely look. What would the queen do?

To Silvermist's amazement, Queen Clarion laughed!

"Well, that cooled me off!" said the queen. Soon everyone was laughing—even Silvermist.

Then Silvermist noticed a five-leaf clover. "Everyone, look!" she called.

"Five-leaf clovers are magic —and lucky!" Fira said. Silvermist picked the clover and tucked it behind her ear.

"It's still your turn, Silvermist," Vidia reminded her.

Silvermist faced the fairies. "I'm not sure if I had bad luck or just a few bad days," she told her friends. "But I do know that if you believe you'll have bad luck, you will."

She turned back to the target and tossed her waterball. *Splash!*

"Bull's-eye!" cried Fira.

"You broke the curse!" Iris said.

Silvermist grinned. "Looks like today is my lucky day!"

Rosetta's Bashful Bloom

"Rosetta! Catch!" Tinker Bell called out.

The garden talent looked up just in time to catch a brand-new watering can.

"Thank you, Tink!" Rosetta called. Her friend waved and flew off. Rosetta quickly filled her new watering can. Her old one had just sprung a leak, so she was glad to have another!

The fairies of Pixie Hollow were very busy preparing to bring fall to the mainland.

Silvermist and the water-talent fairies were learning how to make ice crystals for the first frost. The winter fairies had offered to teach them! Working with another talent always excited Silvermist.

Iridessa and the other light-talent fairies were collecting bright, clear fall sunlight in bottles.

And Fawn was practicing new bedtime stories to tell the baby animals that were going to sleep through the long winter.

As a garden talent, Rosetta usually had to do more work to prepare for the spring and summer seasons on the mainland than for the fall. But this fall, she was as busy as her friends.

There was the usual work in her own garden, such as watering the tulips, singing to the tiger lilies, and complimenting the roses. But on top of all that, Rosetta had a new flower to take care of.

Not too long ago, the Minister of Autumn had given Rosetta a seed wrapped in beautiful red fabric. He wanted her to grow a special fall flower to bring to the mainland.

"This seed will grow an autumn daisy," the minister had said. "I know you'll take good care of this little flower, Rosetta."

"You just leave it up to me!" Rosetta had told the minister with a grin and a wink. "Little daisy-pie and I are going to be best buds, aren't we? Get it? Best . . . *buds*?"

The trip to the mainland was right around the corner. Rosetta should have been happy about bringing the new flower over. But actually, she was a little worried.

The autumn daisy had sprouted quickly. It had grown into a dull green plant with a single yellow flower bud. The plant wasn't tall, and its leaves weren't shiny. It wasn't exactly strange looking, but it wasn't very pretty, either.

It was the most ordinary plant Rosetta had ever raised.

Rosetta was known for growing amazing plants. Her flowers were gorgeous. They were not ordinary.

She let out a frustrated sigh. "I must be doing something wrong," she said.

Rosetta ran through her "Happy Plant Checklist":

Water? Check.

Sunlight? Check.

Rich soil? Check.

Praise? Double check.

Rosetta always praised her plants. She told her forget-me-nots that they were bluer than the summer sky. She told her roses that they were redder than the setting sun. The flowers seemed to perk up at Rosetta's kind words.

But flattery didn't seem to work with the autumn daisy. When Rosetta said, "You smell sweeter than honey," it wilted before her very eyes. And when she told it, "Your blossom will outshine the moon and stars," she could have sworn its single flower bud closed up even tighter.

At this rate, the daisy was never going to be ready for the trip to the mainland. Rosetta didn't want to let the Minister of Autumn or her little bloom down!

That night, Rosetta lay awake in her rose-petal bed. She stared at the ceiling. What was she doing wrong? Why was this one plant so drab when all her other plants were bright and cheerful?

She had been working hard to think up new compliments for the autumn daisy, but each one only seemed to make it sadder.

"Tomorrow I'll figure this out," she promised herself. "I'm going to find a way to make the autumn daisy the prettiest fall-blooming flower the mainland has ever seen."

When the pink light of dawn peeked into Rosetta's bedroom the next morning, she was dressed and ready for the day.

"First," she decided, "I'll see what Iridessa thinks."

Rosetta found her friend in a field of goldenrod. The light fairies were using jars to collect the rays of sunlight that bounced off the golden flowers.

"Tonight, we're going to mix the sunlight with moonlight," Iridessa explained. "This fall, the mainland will have the most golden harvest moon ever!"

Rosetta told Iridessa all about the autumn daisy. "I've tried everything," she said, sighing.

"It sounds like you have," Iridessa agreed. "How can I help?"

"Will you come and look at it, Dess?" Rosetta asked. "Maybe you can tell if it's getting enough sunlight."

"Of course!" Iridessa said. She placed the lid on her jar. Then she flew off to Rosetta's garden.

Iridessa knelt down beside the plant.

"Let's see," the light talent said. She held her hands out over the plant and closed her eyes. A moment later, she opened them again.

"It is getting enough sun. I can feel the energy stored in its leaves," Iridessa said.

"Hmm," Rosetta replied. "Maybe it isn't getting enough water. Let's go ask Silvermist!"

She and Iridessa flew over to the babbling brook, where Silvermist was catching up on the latest fairy gossip. She agreed to take a look at the little flower.

The moment Silvermist saw the plant, she shook her head. "It's getting plenty of water," she said.

"Well," Rosetta said, "if it doesn't need sunshine, and it doesn't need water, then what does it need?"

Just then, they noticed Tink and Fawn flying nearby. Rosetta waved them over.

When Fawn saw the autumn daisy, she shrugged. "It's a little small, but it looks all right," she said.

Tink agreed with Fawn. "The plant seems fine. Are you sure there really is something wrong with it?"

"Just look at it!" Rosetta said impatiently. "It's so . . . so *ordinary*!"

Her friends looked at one another doubtfully.

"And here, watch this!" Rosetta said.

She knelt down in front of the flower. Then she smiled at the plant and said, "When your leaves sway in the breeze, even the most graceful birds look clumsy."

The daisy quivered a bit and then curled itself into a little lump.

Fawn gasped. "It looks like the saddest snail ever," she said. "I've never seen such a bashful little thing."

"See!" Rosetta cried. "Any other plant would be glowing after praise like that." She shook her head. "It's no use. I'm going to have to tell the Minister of Autumn that I failed."

With that, she flew straight to the Autumn Forest.

Rosetta was sorry that the mainland wouldn't get its new plant that fall. She felt bad about disappointing the minister. But she felt even worse about failing the autumn daisy.

When Rosetta arrived at the minister's chambers, she told him the whole story.

"It's getting enough water and enough light," Rosetta said. "And I've been paying it plenty of compliments, too. But they just make things worse! The other day I told the autumn daisy that its leaves were as soft as a kitten's ear, and it actually tried to hide behind a poppy plant."

"Rosetta, fall plants are not like spring or summer plants," the minister said. "Because winter is so close, fall flowers aren't showy or bright like most other flowers. And they can be very, very shy."

"Fawn did say the daisy was bashful," Rosetta said.

"I think all your flattery may be *embarrassing* the daisy," the minister said.

Rosetta gasped. "That's not what I wanted to do!" she said. "I just wanted to make the little daisy-pie happy."

The minister smiled. He gathered some autumn plants in his hands. "Autumn flowers are most happy when they blend into their surroundings," he said. "They work together with the other plants to make the world beautiful as they change color."

When Rosetta got back to her garden, she sat beside the bashful daisy with a handful of autumn plants. "Little daisy-pie, look how well you blend in," she said. "Why, I think you made these other plants more beautiful."

Rosetta beamed as the autumn daisy stood up straighter. Its sturdy leaves bristled proudly. And its flower bud opened just a tiny bit.

"That's the spirit!" Rosetta quietly cheered. "How could I forget that working together makes everything brighter?"

The autumn daisy was finally ready to go to the mainland. And Rosetta had never been more proud of one of her blooms.

A Messy Mystery

One morning, Tinker Bell flew to her workshop. She was eager to begin work on a set of tin measuring spoons. Dulcie, a baking-talent fairy, had dropped them off two nights before.

"The pinch-of-this spoon adds a pinch of *that*," Dulcie had told Tink. "And the add-a-dab spoon is adding a dollop instead. I ruined two batches of pumpkin muffins before I realized!"

Tink had assured her friend that she would get to the bottom of things.

"I bet the spoons need another layer or two of tin added," Tink said as she reached her workshop. With a burst of excitement, she flung open the door.

Tinker Bell gasped. "Blazing copper kettles!" she cried. Her workshop was a mess. Pots and pans and ladles were scattered all over the place.

But worst of all, the measuring spoons weren't where she'd left them. They were gone!

Tink took off for the kitchen. She wondered if Dulcie had come back for the spoons, thinking they were finished.

When she got there, Tinker Bell's mouth dropped open in surprise. "Dulcie, what's going on?" she asked.

"Someone made a mess!" Dulcie said. "And what's worse,

the gingerbread cupcakes I made are gone!"

Tinker Bell looked around. She spotted a trail of crumbs leading to the door of the Tea Room.

"Follow me!" she told Dulcie.

When Tink and
Dulcie reached the
Tea Room, they could
hardly believe what
they saw.

The Tea Room was
a mess, too! And where
the trail of cupcake
crumbs ended, a trail of
sugar began.

"Look!" Dulcie said.
"The silver sugar shaker is missing. I put it here this morning!"

"Who is making this mess?" asked Prilla, a clapping talent.
"Things are being turned upside down all over Pixie Hollow!"

"Someone has to solve this messy mystery," Tink said,
pointing at the trail of sugar. "Prilla, will you help me?"

The sugar led out into the hall. It continued through the corridors and even went up the stairs!

"I can't believe this," Tink said as she and Prilla followed the sugary mess.

"Who do you think did it?" Prilla asked.

"I have no idea," Tink replied.

"Do you think it was a fairy?" Prilla continued. "Or maybe—"

"Beck!" Tink interrupted, coming to a halt. Prilla couldn't stop in time! She flew into Tink's back, and Tink stumbled forward.

"What?" Prilla said.

Tink pointed. The two fairies had followed the trail of sugar from the Tea Room all the way to Beck's door.

Beck was an animal-talent fairy and one of Tink's good friends.

"What in Never Land would make Beck leave such a mess?" Tink wondered aloud.

The door to Beck's room was open just a crack. Tink and Prilla peered inside. Beck was nowhere in sight, but Tink spotted something glinting in the sunlight streaming through the window.

"Dulcie's measuring spoons!" Tink cried. She pushed open the door and flew into the room. "Why does Beck have these?"

Prilla flew to another corner. "Look, Tink," she said, "the sugar shaker."

Tink tugged on her bangs. Could Beck really have taken the spoons and the sugar shaker and made all those messes?

"Come on," Tink said, "we have to find Beck."

Tink and Prilla flew all over Pixie Hollow looking for Beck. She wasn't in the meadow with the field mice or at Havendish Stream with the water fairies.

Suddenly, Tink and Prilla spotted Bess, an art-talent fairy, fluttering around her studio. She looked upset.

"Look at this mess!" Bess cried when Tink and Prilla flew up. "My paints are all over the floor, and the cake I was painting has disappeared!"

Prilla comforted Bess while Tink looked around the studio.

Finally, Tink turned to Bess. "We'll get to the bottom of this messy mystery," she said. She gave her friend a warm smile. Then she took off. Prilla chased after her.

"Why would Beck make a mess in Bess's art studio?" Prilla asked.

"I don't know," Tink replied. The two fairies flew across a clearing and into a meadow filled with flowers.

"Why would she eat the cake Bess was painting?" Prilla asked.

"I don't know!" Tink snapped.

She watched Prilla shrink back in shock. Tink's glow flared orange with embarrassment. She knew Prilla was only trying to help. But she couldn't answer the questions the young fairy was asking!

"Prilla . . ." Tink began to apologize.

"Caught you!" Beck yelled as she flew up over some flowers.

Tink and Prilla jumped in surprise. "Beck!" Tink cried. "We've been looking all over for you."

"You have?" Beck asked. "Why?"

"There's a mess-maker in Pixie Hollow," Prilla said. "We followed the trail to you."

Beck began to laugh. "You've been following me, and I've been following *them*!" She pointed to the ground below where Tink and Prilla were hovering.

To Tink and Prilla's amazement, three baby hedgehogs came rolling out of the grass.

"We were playing hide-and-seek, but these little guys kept running away," Beck explained. "I tracked them all over Pixie Hollow before I finally caught up with them. I thought I could handle them on my own, but they're too much for just one fairy!"

"We can help," Prilla offered.

The three fairies worked together to build a space for the baby hedgehogs to play in.

"Now you can keep an eye on them while they have fun!" Prilla said, smiling.

"And best of all, we solved the messy mystery!" Tink said.

The fairies giggled and settled down to watch the hedgehog babies play.

The Fairy Flood

Rani, a water-talent fairy, hummed to herself as she hurried down the stairs. She was on her way to see her friend Tinker Bell. Rani wasn't looking where she was going. She didn't notice anything unusual until—*splash*!

Rani looked down. Her feet were covered with water!

"Oh, my!" Rani exclaimed as a teapot floated by. "The dishes are floating away!"

"The dishes aren't the only things floating away," Dulcie called out. The baking-talent fairy paddled toward Rani in a large pot. "All of Pixie Hollow is flooded!"

Before Rani could respond, she and Dulcie heard a fairy outside cry, "Help!"

"It sounds like someone is in trouble!" Rani said. She leaped into Dulcie's pot, and the two fairies paddled out the door.

Lily, a garden-talent fairy, was trying to rescue a nest of baby birds that had fallen into the water.

"The nest is too heavy!" Lily cried. "Can you help me pull it in?"

Rani and Dulcie grabbed on to the branch Lily was holding. The three fairies pulled the chicks to safety.

Lily breathed a sigh of relief. "That was close," she said.

Rani nodded. She looked down at Dulcie's pot. It reminded her of something.

"Oh! I completely forgot—I have to go see Tink," Rani exclaimed. "Dulcie, can I borrow your pot and spoon?"

"Sure," Dulcie said.

Rani climbed into the pot.

"There's a dent in one of the handles," Dulcie called as Rani began to paddle away. "Would you ask—"

"Tink if she'll fix it? I'm sure she'd love to!" Rani waved and paddled off.

Rani arrived at Tink's workshop and knocked on the door. When Tink opened it, three fish leaped inside.

"These fish keep trying to jump into my pots and pans!" Tink cried. "I can't get any work done."

Rani spotted a shiny silver spoon. "How about a distraction?"

Tink dangled the spoon in the water. The fish swam around it.

Just then, Spring, a message-talent fairy, arrived. "Beck is looking for you," she told Rani. "She said it's urgent."

Rani climbed into Spring's boat. "Oh, Tink," she called back, "Dulcie's pot has a dent in the handle. Can you fix it for her?"

As Spring paddled away from Tink's workshop, Rani looked around. There was water as far as she could see!

Rani wondered where all the water was coming from. As a water-talent fairy, she knew her friends would be looking for her to help solve the problem.

Just then, Rani's friend Terence flew up. He was a dust-keeper. Rani thought she might be able to clear some of the water if she had a little more pixie dust.

Before Rani could ask, though, Terence said, "The pixie dust is all wet!"

Spring and Terence started talking about how the fairies would get around Pixie Hollow to do their work. Rani looked behind her and saw a group of water-talent fairies floating in leaf boats. One of the fairies reached out and touched the water. A fountain shot three feet into the air. The other water talents began setting off fountains, too.

Rani was happy to see at least one talent group enjoying the flood. She wanted to stay and make fountains as well, but she knew Beck was waiting for her.

Spring and Terence were still discussing their plans, so Rani borrowed a leaf boat from another water talent. She paddled and paddled. It seemed there was no end to the flood of water! Suddenly, she heard someone calling her.

"Rani! Rani, there you are!"

Turning, Rani saw Beck riding on the back of a turtle.

"I know what's causing the flood!" Beck said. "Come on, I'll show you!"

The two fairies set off. Soon they arrived at a giant dam. The dam was keeping all the water in Pixie Hollow!

"Hello!" Beck said in Beaver. There was a splash, and three brown heads poked out of the water.

Beck chattered to the beavers. Then she turned to Rani. "They don't want to move," she said. "It took them a long time to find the perfect spot."

Rani thought for a moment. "Tell them I know a better spot!"

Beck told the beavers what Rani had said. They were quiet for a few minutes. Then they smacked their tails against the water.

"That's a yes!" Beck exclaimed.

The next day, the beavers moved their dam. The water began to recede, and soon, the bright sun dried out Pixie Hollow. The green grass stood up tall. The flowers and plants stretched toward the sun's rays.

Rani walked around Pixie Hollow, helping any fairy she could. The pixie dust was dry, and Terence had given all the water-talent fairies an extra scoop so they could help clean up the floodwaters.

Tinker Bell was standing beside a leaf boat that was floating in a puddle. Rani noticed that her friend looked a little sad.

"What's wrong, Tink?" Rani asked. "Aren't you happy that Pixie Hollow is back to normal?"

"I guess so," Tink said with a sigh. "But I kind of miss those little fish. They were good company! And traveling by leaf boat was fun, too."

Rani smiled. Some other fairies had told her the same thing! "Come with me," she told Tink.

Rani led Tinker Bell to a small cove off Havendish Stream. Tink gasped in delight!

There, fairies of all talents paddled in leaf boats and played with the fish.

Rani smiled. The flood had made things difficult. But she was glad to see that the other fairies had found ways to have fun with

water. She loved her talent—and it was even better when she could share it with her friends!

The Fairy Campout

Tinker Bell was resting on a bright red rose in the meadow. The tinker fairy had finished fixing all the pots and pans in her workshop. Now she was trying to plan her next adventure.

"I played fairy tag yesterday," she said. "And Fawn wants to play pea shoot tomorrow."

She didn't know what to do with her afternoon!

Suddenly, a delicious scent tickled her nose. A cooking-talent fairy was roasting chestnuts. That gave Tink an idea.

"I'll go on a campout!" she cried.

Tink flew to the kitchen, where she found her friend Dulcie.

"I'm going on a campout, and I need to pack some food," she told the baking talent.

"What's a campout?" asked Dulcie.

"It's when you make a home away from home," Tink explained. "You pitch a tent, build a fire, and cook dinner, all outside under the stars."

Dulcie's eyes sparkled with excitement. "Can I come, too?" she asked.

"Of course!" Tink exclaimed. "All fairies are welcome!"

Word of Tink's latest adventure quickly spread through Pixie Hollow. Fairies of all talents gathered leaf blankets and filled packs with their belongings.

Tink was waiting in the courtyard when everyone arrived. "Are you all ready?" she asked.

"Ready!" the fairies cried.

"Wait for me!" someone called out.

Tink turned around and saw Dulcie. She was carrying the biggest leaf pack Tink had ever seen.

"What's in that pack?" Tink asked.

"All my baking things!" Dulcie replied. "I can't imagine making a home away from home without them." Dulcie hefted the pack onto her back. "Are we ready to go?"

Tink shrugged. "We're all set," she said.

Tinker Bell flew up to the front of the crowd. "Let's go!" she called out.

The fairies zigzagged through the forest, looking for the perfect spot to set up camp. But they couldn't agree! The water fairies wanted to camp near Havendish Stream, while the forest fairies wanted to pitch their tents deep in the woods.

While the fairies discussed where to go, Dulcie set down her heavy pack. "Can't we just stop here?" she said, panting.

But Tink just shook her head. "I know the perfect place," she said. "Come on!"

Tink led the fairies to a pretty, sunlit clearing.

"It's close to the forest *and* the stream," she said. "And best of all, we can gaze up at the stars!"

"This *is* the perfect spot!" Prilla exclaimed. She set down her leaf pack and started to make camp. The other fairies joined her.

While Fira and the light talents made friends with the local fireflies, the other fairies pitched their tents in a circle. Then they built a giant campfire.

A group of forest-talent fairies set off to search the surrounding area for food. They returned to the camp with loads of berries, and even found some large chestnuts to roast over the fire.

"Brass buckles!" Tink exclaimed when she saw the chestnuts. "Those will be delicious."

As the sun set, the fairies began to prepare their dinner. A cooking talent roasted chestnuts over the fire. Prilla plucked ripe strawberries from the vine. The fairy campout was under way!

"Mmm," Rani said, taking another bite. "I've never had a better dinner."

Tink looked around the campsite. Everyone was having a wonderful time. But Tinker Bell couldn't help feeling that something was missing.

Suddenly, Tink snapped her fingers. "That's it!" she crowed. "We need to tell campfire stories!"

The fairies gathered around the fire, and a storytelling talent began. "Once upon a time, there was a ladybug who loved to dance—"

"No!" Tink interrupted. "Campfire stories have to be scary!"

"Scary?" Beck asked.

Tink smiled wide. "The scarier the better."

Suddenly, Beck flew up in front of the crowd. "I know a scary story!" she said. "It's about a snake with two heads."

Beck raised her arms, and the shadow of a two-headed snake appeared on the rock wall behind her.

"Oh, I know one, too!" Bess said. She leaped up from her seat and spread her arms wide. "It's about the ghost of an owl."

The fairies gasped. They took turns telling scary stories until everyone's wings shook.

Tink grinned. "I know the scariest story ever!"

She leaned close to the fire. "It's about a wicked, smelly . . . pirate!"

"Ooh." The fairies shuddered.

"And that's not all," Tink went on. "At the end of his arm was a huge metal hook!"

Clank! Crash!

"Ahh!" yelled the fairies. They jumped up from their seats and flew to their tents.

"What was that? Is someone out there? Why did we tell so many scary stories?" they asked all at once.

Tink quickly lit a torch. She crept quietly to the edge of the campsite.

Tink saw a shadow just beyond their camp. She flew closer and closer until she came face-to-face with . . .

"Dulcie!" Tink cried. "Where have you been?"

"I got lost," Dulcie said. She set down her heavy leaf pack. "It took me ages to find the campsite. Did I miss all the fun?"

Dulcie looked around in surprise. "Hey! Where is everyone?" she asked.

"They're hiding," Tinker Bell said. She told Dulcie about the scary stories they had told. "Beck told us about a two-headed snake, and Bess scared everyone with a story about a ghost owl. I was just starting my story when we heard a strange noise. Everyone went to hide in their tents."

"Well," Dulcie said, "I think I can fix that."

In no time at all, Dulcie had whipped up a special campfire cake. Even the most frightened fairies couldn't resist the delicious smell.

Tink helped Dulcie carry the cake to the center of the campsite.

"I told you I couldn't make a home away from home without my baking things," Dulcie said as the fairies dug in.

Tink smiled. "The campout wouldn't have been as sweet without you, Dulcie."

Lady Fawn

"That was an incredible catch you made out there," Fawn declared. She smiled at the little gray field mouse trotting just behind her. "I've never had so much fun!"

The mouse lifted up a tiny muddy paw and gave Fawn a high five. He and his field-mouse friends had just finished an exciting game of fairy football.

Fawn loved being an animal-talent fairy. Her favorite part was playing rough-and-tumble games with her animal friends.

"What did you say?" Fawn asked, listening closely as the mice chattered away. "Sure! I would love to have another game soon!" she exclaimed.

Fawn giggled as the mice scampered home for lunch. She felt her stomach rumble. All that action on the field had worked up her appetite, too.

"Hmmm, maybe I'll see if there are any blueberry waffles left in the kitchen," she told herself as she flew into the center of Pixie Hollow.

Fairies of all talents were busy in the courtyard. "I wonder what's going on," Fawn said.

Suddenly, Fawn's eyes widened. "The tea party! I forgot!"

A group of harvest fairies were carrying baskets of bright red strawberries. A light-talent fairy was adding rays of sunlight to a pink punch bowl. Several hummingbirds were working with decoration-talent fairies, draping tables with grapevines.

Two summer-rain fairies waved to Fawn.

"Welcome back!" she called to them.

The seasonal talents had just returned from bringing summer to the mainland. Queen Clarion and the Minister of Summer wanted to celebrate their hard work with a tea party for all the Never fairies and their animal friends.

"There you are," Rosetta said as she flew over to Fawn. As usual, the garden fairy looked beautiful. She was wearing a pink rose-petal dress and carrying a basket of bright blue forget-me-nots. "Let me guess," she said, taking in Fawn's muddy pants. "Leapfrog? Or was it hide-and-seek this time?"

Fawn laughed. "No, fairy football! You should play sometime, Rosetta. It's so much fun!"

"Not to mention dirty! I'm just not one for horsing around, Fawn. Can you imagine me all covered with mud?" Rosetta shivered, then gave her friend a warm smile. "In fact, I can't imagine *you* all prim and proper for the tea party!"

Rosetta stuck a blue forget-me-not into Fawn's hair. Then she flew off.

Fawn looked down at herself. She was covered with mud. Her pants had a rip above one knee. Prickly thistles were stuck to her hair.

Fawn wondered if Rosetta was right. She did like to horse around quite a bit. But was she *too* rough-and-tumble?

Fawn hurried home to get cleaned up. She slipped off her muddy shoes at the door. Then she opened her wardrobe.

There were a few pairs of pants woven from dandelion fluff and some soft thistledown shirts. She knew these would be perfectly fine to wear to the tea party. But she wanted to be ladylike, too.

"And who better to help me than Rosetta!" she said.

She grabbed a set of clean clothes from her wardrobe and took off for Rosetta's house.

Rosetta was outside, scattering flower petals around her doorway when Fawn flew up.

"Rosetta," Fawn called out, "can you help me get ready for the tea party? I'd like to try to be . . . prim and proper. Like you!"

"Of course!" Rosetta said with a wide smile. She looked Fawn over from wingtip to toe. "First we have to clean off all that mud. Then we'll find you a dress. If you're going to be a lady, you should wear flowers, not weeds." She plucked Fawn's clothes from her hands and dropped them beside the door. Then she led her friend inside.

Fawn sat in front of Rosetta's dressing table. A ladybug was perched atop the mirror. "It's not hard to be a lady, is it?" Fawn asked.

The ladybug shook her head and grinned.

Fawn smiled. Then she settled back in her chair and let Rosetta get to work.

When Rosetta had pulled all the twigs and leaves from Fawn's hair, she smiled. "Now, there's a bubble bath with your name on it!" she said.

Fawn wrinkled her nose. Since the day she'd arrived, she'd disliked wing-washing time. But Rosetta wouldn't take no for an answer. She hurried Fawn into the tub. Then she poured lavender bubble bath into the warm water.

Once Fawn was cleaned up, Rosetta gave her a beautiful dress made of tulip petals.

"I'm not sure this is for me," Fawn said as she looked at her reflection in the mirror. "It's so . . . dainty."

"This is what ladies wear! The color is perfect for you," Rosetta said. She tucked a pink pansy into Fawn's hair, which had been twisted into a fancy braid.

"You do want to be a lady, don't you?" the ladybug chimed in.

Fawn looked at the dress again. Then she nodded firmly. She took the soft lily slippers Rosetta offered and put them on. "If this is what it takes, I'll do it."

Now that Fawn *looked* like a lady, Rosetta wanted to teach her how to *act* like one, too. She took out two teacups and filled them with lemonade. She handed one to Fawn.

"Now, when you take a sip of tea, you want to hold your cup like so," Rosetta said. She wrapped her fingers around the handle but left her pinkie sticking up.

Fawn tried to hold the cup like Rosetta had shown her. But the teacup tipped, and she spilled lemonade down the front of her dress.

"Don't worry," Rosetta said. "Practice makes perfect. Let's try a curtsy next."

"A curtsy?" Fawn asked.

The ladybug stood up, held her wings out on both sides, and bent slightly forward.

Fawn picked up her dress, crossed her left leg behind her right one, and bowed. I did it! she thought—just before she lost her balance and tumbled to the floor.

After a few more unsuccessful tries, Fawn shrugged sadly. "Maybe I'm not meant to be a lady," she said. "I can only be me."

"That's it, Fawn!" Rosetta exclaimed. She took her friend's hand, and they flew to the meadow where Fawn had played football. A few of the field mice were still there.

Rosetta asked Fawn to explain to the mice what they were doing. The animals were eager to help!

Fawn practiced walking gracefully by balancing a piece of bark on her head as she raced a mouse across the field. Then she tried another curtsy as she leaned down to touch noses with the smallest of the mice. He squeaked happily.

"Even Queen Clarion would be impressed," Rosetta said.

Finally, it was time for the tea party. All the fairies gathered in the courtyard dressed in their fairy best.

"Come on," Rosetta whispered to Fawn. "You're ready."

The two fairies approached the table where their friends were already sitting.

"Rosetta, who's your friend?" Tinker Bell asked. Then she looked more closely at Fawn. "Blazing copper kettles!" She gasped. "Fawn, is that you?"

"Fawn, you look lovely!" Silvermist said.

Fawn's glow flared brighter as her friends admired her dress and slippers.

Fawn told her friends how Rosetta had taught her to be a lady. As she came to the part where Rosetta had called on the field mice for help, she overheard something that made her ears perk up.

"We discovered a new game while we were on the mainland," a summer-rain fairy said. "The Clumsies call it baseball."

"A new game?" Fawn said, her eyes lighting up with excitement. The summer-rain fairy was already putting together two teams to try out the game.

Fawn looked down at her delicate petal dress. Then she turned to Rosetta with a hopeful smile. "What do you think?" she asked. "Can we play?"

Rosetta grinned. "Who says a lady can't have fun?"

Fawn sprang up from her seat. She was quickly followed by her friends. They listened carefully to the rules. Then, using acorn caps for bases, twigs for bats, and acorns for balls, the Never fairies played their first-ever game of baseball.

"That was the best!" Fawn said after the game. She took a big bite of strawberry-seed cake.

The game had ended in a tie, and now all the fairies were enjoying the tea party.

Rosetta blew a stray piece of hair off her face. "I guess I don't always have to look perfect!"

"No one minds a little messiness now and then," Queen Clarion said as she came up behind them.

Fawn wiped a crumb from her flushed cheek. Then she passed a tray of blackberry tarts to Rosetta. "Would you like one?"

Rosetta winked. "After you, Fawn. Ladies first!"

Vidia's Snowy Surprise

Vidia, a fast-flying fairy, loved to make fun of the other fairies' talents. She thought her talent made her better than everyone else.

One day, Vidia was so mean to a water fairy who was making fountains in Havendish Stream that the fairy began to cry.

Tinker Bell had seen the whole thing. She was furious!

"Someday you'll learn to appreciate another talent!" Tink yelled angrily.

Vidia just laughed. "Darling, that won't happen until it snows in Pixie Hollow," she said.

As Tink watched Vidia fly away, she swore she'd make Vidia be nice someday.

Word of Vidia's announcement quickly spread. The fairies were discouraged. They knew it would never snow in Pixie Hollow. And that meant Vidia would never change her mean ways.

A garden talent named Lily was tending her plants one day when she started to get cold. She shivered as she inspected her violets, and she shivered more when she checked on her bush with the bright red berries.

She rubbed her arms. "Why is it so chilly outside?" she said.

207

Just then, Lily noticed something strange falling from the sky. She caught one of the objects in her hand. It was cold and melted in her palm.

"Snow?" Lily said. She looked up at the sky. More crystal flakes fell around her.

"Lily!" Rosetta, another garden talent, called out to her. "Can you believe this? It's snowing in Pixie Hollow!"

Rosetta held out her hands to catch some flakes. They melted as quickly in her hands as they had in Lily's.

"I was by Havendish Stream with Rani when I saw the first flakes," Rosetta explained. "I flew here as fast as I could to make sure the gardens would be all right."

Lily nodded. It had never snowed in Pixie Hollow before, and the garden talents didn't know how their plants would fare.

"What in Never Land is going on?" Lily mumbled as she watched the snow fall.

Before long, a thin layer of white covered the ground. All the fairies came out to play in the snow.

Dulcie, a baking-talent fairy, caught a flake on her tongue. "Hmm," she said, "it's rather bland." She'd hoped the crystals would taste as sweet and sugary as they looked.

As the day went on, the snow continued to fall. Soon it came up to the fairies' knees. Everyone shivered, but they were so excited to see snow in Pixie Hollow that they didn't want to go inside.

Prilla scooped up a handful of snow and shaped it into a ball. With a twinkle in her eye, she tossed it at her friend Tinker Bell.

Tink laughed. "Watch out, Prilla!" she called. "I'll get you back!"

Soon, more fairies joined in the snowball fight. They laughed as they darted to and fro, trying to avoid the cold snowballs flying through the air.

Soon the fairies grew too cold to stay outside. The sewing talents set to work making hats and scarves and jackets. The shoemaking fairies made boots lined with dandelion fluff. The fairies loved their new fashions. And they kept them warm enough to play for hours!

By now, the snow was wing-deep. The art-talent fairies had discovered a new use for it!

"You can sculpt snow!" Bess told Tink. She'd built a perfect snow fairy, complete with wings made from sheets of frosted spiderwebs. The snow fairy looked remarkably like Tinker Bell!

At Havendish Stream, the water-talent fairies gathered together. The usually bubbling stream was now as smooth as glass.

Rani tapped her foot on the ice. "Look," she said. "It's hard and slippery, too." She stepped out onto the surface and started gliding across it.

"Come on!" she called to the others. "This is more fun than water-skating!"

The other water talents joined Rani. When they water-skated, they moved with the waves in the stream and splashed across the surface. But ice-skating was so fast!

"I feel like I'm flying!" a water talent cried. "But I'm not moving my wings at all. See? Not even a flutter!" She laughed as she raced across the ice.

Soon the other talents joined in. It wasn't quite as easy for them as it was for the water talents, but it wasn't hard, either. Everyone was having a great time.

Everyone . . . including Vidia! The fast-flying talents were racing down the hillsides on leaf sleds.

Vidia could never say no to a race. She zipped ahead of the others. "You can't catch me, darlings!" she shouted.

Terence, a dust-keeper fairy, pushed Tink along the snowy bank near the stream in a silver spoon.

"Faster, Terence, faster!" Tink cried.

Terence beat his wings as hard as he could. He pushed the spoon with all his might and then let go.

Tink went sailing down the snowy hill. "Blazing copper kettles!" she yelled. "I love snow!"

Tink slid to a stop beside Rani and Vidia.

"Well, Vidia," Rani said. "Now you have to be nice to all the other talents."

"Whatever do you mean?" Vidia asked.

"You said that you'd appreciate another talent when it snowed in Pixie Hollow," Tink reminded her.

Vidia sniffed. "I suppose I could . . . if I didn't have better things to do." And with a flip of her ponytail, she flew away.

Tink and Rani watched Vidia hop into her leaf sled.

"You know," Tink said, "I think Vidia does appreciate the other talents. Or she wouldn't be having this much fun!"

"And neither would we," Rani said. The two fairies smiled at each other and flew off to play in the snow with their friends.

Spring Cleaning

Tinker Bell was hard at work in the highest branches of a tall oak tree. She had just tapped the last nail into place on a new invention. She flew back to admire her work.

"My new wind spinner looks good," Tink said to herself. "But does it work?"

Just then, a breeze blew through the leaves of the tree. The gust was so strong, Tink had to flutter her wings as fast as she could to stay near the tree.

She smiled and took a deep, satisfied breath as she watched her new invention twirl.

"Blazing copper kettles!" she exclaimed. "It's the Spring Breeze!"

The Spring Breeze swept through Pixie Hollow, rousing the other fairies. It was time for spring cleaning!

Fairies of all talents set to work scrubbing their homes from top to bottom.

Tink was on her way back to her workshop when she heard someone call her name.

"Tink! Down here!"

Tink saw her friend Lily below her. The garden fairy was planting flowers.

"Could you help me water these flower beds?" Lily asked. "I forgot to bring some seedlings from my garden. I'll be back in just a moment."

Tink looked at the rows and rows of new flowers, then back at Lily's one watering can, which dripped a drop of water at a time. *Drip, drip, drip.*

"Sure, I can help!" Tink said.

As soon as Lily flew off, Tinker Bell rigged up a new sprinkler system. She strung a few more watering cans on a vine and pulled. The cans tipped, showering the flowers with water.

Lily was hurrying back to her garden when a water talent named Rani stopped her.

"Oh, Lily," Rani said. "Could you do me a favor?"

"Of course!" Lily replied.

Rani pointed to a stream of soapy water. "I've run out of soap and can't finish washing. Could you keep an eye on things here? I'll only be a minute!"

Lily nodded. She'd be back to her flowers in no time.

Lily watched the bubbles floating past. If the bubbles were bigger, Rani could get the washing done faster, Lily thought to herself.

"Come on, bubbles," Lily encouraged. "Get bigger! I know you can!" She sprinkled some pixie dust over the bubbles, and they began to grow.

Rani was on her way to the laundry room for more soap when she spotted her friend Beck, an animal talent.

"What in Never Land are you doing?" Rani asked.

"The squirrels are helping me dust!" Beck said. "I'm glad you're here, Rani. Would you keep an eye on these guys for a minute while I go find them a snack? We've been working all morning."

Rani happily agreed.

Rani watched the squirrels while Beck flew off. She pointed out spots that still needed to be dusted. But the squirrels weren't paying attention.

The water talent frowned. She wished she could speak Squirrel like Beck. "*Cheee! Cheee!*" Rani said, trying to imitate her friend.

The squirrels froze.

"It worked!" Rani exclaimed. "*Cheee! Cheee!*" Rani said again.

The squirrels began to move quickly. They turned over tables and chairs. They ripped the curtains off the windows.

"No!" Rani cried. "Stop! Please, don't do that! *Cheee! Cheee!*"

"What's going on?" Beck asked as she flew into the room. She gasped when she saw the mess the squirrels were making. "Rani, what happened?"

"I was telling them where to dust," Rani said. "I told them in Squirrel, like you do, Beck."

Beck's eyes grew wide. "Rani, what did you say in Squirrel, exactly?" she asked slowly.

"*Cheee! Cheee!*" Rani said. The squirrels ran faster.

"That doesn't mean *dust*!" Beck cried. "That means *hawk*!"

Beck tried to calm the squirrels. But they were too frightened. They ran in circles around the room. Then, one of them bolted out into the courtyard. The other two chased after him.

Rani and Beck hurried to keep up.

When they reached the courtyard, the squirrels skidded through the soapy water.

"Oh, no!" Lily yelled. The huge bubbles she'd made were floating everywhere.

The squirrels couldn't stop. They slipped and slid toward Tink's sprinkler vine.

"Look out!" Tinker Bell cried.

But it was too late. *Crash!* The squirrels slid into the sprinkler system. They lay in a wet, sudsy mess, tangled up in the vine.

Tinker Bell, Lily, Rani, and Beck looked at the courtyard. It was full of soggy laundry, soapy flowers, and a lot of very upset fairies.

"Look at this mess!" a laundry-talent fairy yelled. "It's worse than when we started this morning!"

Tink, Lily, Rani, and Beck felt terrible. "I'd fly backward if I could," Rani said. "I didn't mean to scare the squirrels."

"I shouldn't have made the bubbles grow," Lily said.

"I probably used too much water," Tink said. She tugged on her bangs.

Rani reached for a moss mop. Then she passed one to Beck.

"Where do we even start?" Beck asked.

The other fairies' angry looks softened. Slowly, all the fairies went back to their cleanup tasks.

Rani and Beck mopped up the extra water. Tink and Lily set to work replanting flowers. It took all day, but finally Pixie Hollow sparkled from top to bottom.

"I love spring cleaning," Rani said, admiring their work.

"And best of all, we don't have to do it again until next year!" Tink said with a smile.

The Diamond-Dust Snowflake

"**B**lazing copper kettles!" Tinker Bell exclaimed, a grin stretching across her face. "The Minister of Winter has asked me to make Queen Clarion a gift for this winter!"

Silvermist, a water-talent fairy, joined the other fairies clustered around Tink. "What are you going to make?" she asked.

Tink tugged on her bangs. "That's the problem," she said. "I don't know!"

"You could make a sleigh," Rosetta suggested.

"Queen Clarion already has one," Tink replied.

"How about snowshoes?" asked Fawn.

Tink frowned. "That's not right for a queen."

Silvermist thought of the winter fairies with a pang of envy. Being a water talent was great. She loved going to the mainland at the end of each winter to scatter morning dewdrops and make bubbling fountains in newly thawed streams. But the winter fairies got to make *snow*, carefully crafting each and every flake.

Suddenly, Silvermist had an idea. "You could make the queen a special snowflake in honor of winter," she said.

Tink's wings fluttered so hard, she lifted into the air. "That's it, Sil!" she cried. "A special snowflake as pretty as lace. And I know just what to use!" Tink took off like a jackrabbit.

Silvermist spent the afternoon at Havendish Stream, practicing her water fountains. But she thought about Tink and her snowflake for the queen the whole time.

All of a sudden, Tink flew toward her. "Silvermist! Look!" Tink called. In her hands was a rock-crystal bottle. "I wanted to show you, since it was your idea!"

Tink held out the bottle. It was filled with sparkling material. A ray of sunshine caught the bottle and it shone like a thousand stars. Silvermist blinked repeatedly—the light was so bright!

"It's diamond dust!" Tink said. "The mining talents found it. Won't it make a beautiful snowflake?"

"I just wish I knew more about snowflakes," Tink went on. "Diamond dust is so precious. What if I mess up?"

"You need to see more snowflakes, Tink," Silvermist said. "You should go to the Winter Woods! I'll go with you!"

"Yes!" Tink cried.

The Winter Woods were colder than cold. Tink and Silvermist bundled up in coats of finely spun spiders' thread. They put on boots and mittens lined with dandelion fluff. Finally the two fairies set off.

When they arrived in the Winter Woods, they were cheerfully greeted by the winter fairies. Silvermist flew in close to one of the fairies, who was shaping a snowflake. It looked like a frost blossom. Next to it was a large pile of finished snowflakes.

Silvermist took off her mitten and picked one up. The snowflake was a work of art. But unlike water, the snowflake in her hand was very cold. It made her shiver.

"Can you give me some pointers?" Tink asked the winter fairies. "I'm making a snowflake out of diamond dust for the queen!" She pulled the crystal bottle from her sleeve.

"You brought the diamond dust?" Silvermist asked, shocked.

Tink shrugged. "I didn't want to leave it at home."

The winter fairies eagerly taught Tink and Silvermist about the different snowflake shapes—the starburst, the rose, and the sparkler. They even showed the two fairies how to carve each of the shapes.

"But it's not all work here in the Winter Woods," one of the fairies said with a grin.

"It's not?" Tink asked.

"No." The fairy giggled. Then, quick as a flash, she grabbed a handful of snow and threw it at Tink.

Tink wiped the snow from her face. Then she launched her own snowball at Silvermist! Soon, a full-on snowball fight raged.

Finally, tuckered out, Silvermist fell back into the snow. The other fairies were settling down, too. Moving her legs and arms, Silvermist lazily made a snow fairy. Tink fluttered over to sit beside her.

"You'll have no problem making the diamond-dust snowflake now," Silvermist said to Tink.

"Yes, my snowflake will be beautiful," Tink said with a happy sigh. She reached into her sleeve for the crystal bottle. But it wasn't there.

Tink jumped to her feet and whirled around. The bottle lay several wingbeats away on its side in the snow. She flew to it. The cork had come out, and the bottle was empty!

Silvermist hurried over to Tink. All around her, the snow glittered in the sunlight. But was it snow, or was it diamond dust?

"Oh, Silvermist, what am I going to do?" Tink wailed.

One by one, the winter fairies came over to Tink and Silvermist. They looked sadly at the empty bottle and then at the glittering snow.

"Can't you sort out the diamond dust from the snow?" Silvermist asked their new friends.

The winter fairies frowned. "I don't think so," one said at last.

"I could use a magnet!" Tink shouted. But her determined look vanished when she realized that diamond dust, unlike the metals she usually worked with, wasn't magnetic.

But Tink's outburst had gotten Silvermist thinking. Water fairies attracted water to themselves, just like magnets drew iron. And what was snow, after all, but frozen water?

If the winter fairies could melt the snow in the spot where Tink had spilled the dust, Silvermist would be able to pull the water away. Then Tink could collect the diamond dust.

It might not work, but they had to try.

Silvermist shared her idea with the winter fairies. She'd need their help to melt the snowflakes in this part of the clearing. Tink would have to gather the diamond dust quickly once Silvermist lifted the water away.

"Yes," one of the winter fairies said. She nodded eagerly as the idea sank in. "I think that would work!"

The winter fairies formed a circle around the spot where the bottle had fallen. In the center of the circle, Tink fluttered beside Silvermist.

"Do you really think—" Tink started.

"We're going to try," Silvermist assured her with a small but hopeful smile.

The winter fairies linked hands and shut their eyes. Slowly, the snow at their feet began to melt. Silvermist raised her arms and drew the water upward. As Tinker Bell watched, it lifted off the ground and whirled above their heads, a watery spiral of melted snow!

"Aha!" Tink cried. She dove toward the ground, which was now free of snow. The diamond dust sparkled as brightly as a lost gem. She swept up the pieces and funneled them back into the

crystal bottle. Then she stuffed the cork firmly back in the bottle.

"She's done!" the water fairy called to the winter fairies. Suddenly Silvermist felt a shift in the air. As she watched, the water swirling above her head changed into thousands of little snowflakes. The snow fell on the fairies' upturned faces.

Tinker Bell and Silvermist thanked the winter fairies. Then they raced back to the meadow.

Tink vanished into her workshop for three days. At last she emerged. She flew straight to Silvermist. Diamond dust sparkled on her cheeks and in her hair.

"Look," she said in a whisper. She held out the diamond-dust snowflake. It glittered in the sunlight.

"Tink, it's beautiful!" Silvermist exclaimed.

Tink hugged Silvermist. "I couldn't have done it without you," she said. "The snowflake was your idea. You went with me to the woods. And you saved the lost diamond dust! This is *your* gift to the queen as much as it is mine."

That evening, Silvermist and Tinker Bell presented their gift to Queen Clarion.

"By the Second Star!" the queen exclaimed. "I've never seen such a snowflake. However did you make this?"

Tinker Bell smiled, then nudged Silvermist forward. "With a little help from the best water-talent fairy in Pixie Hollow!" Tink cried.

Silvermist's heart skipped happily. How had she ever thought anything could be better than being a water-talent fairy? She had the best talent in the world!

Lost Things

One day, Tinker Bell was flying over Havendish Stream, heading back to her workshop. Suddenly, she caught sight of something strange. It was stuck beneath a large branch sticking out of the water.

The fairies often found interesting and useful items in Havendish Stream or washed up on Never Land's shores. Tink was always on the hunt for these lost items. She used them to fix things around Pixie Hollow and to invent new gadgets.

Tinker Bell balanced herself on the branch and pulled with all her might. Finally, the thing came loose. It was as tall as Tink and had a bunch of prickly bristles sticking out of one end. She had never seen anything like it. Tink tugged on her bangs. She couldn't think of a single use for the object. "All that work for nothing!" she grumbled.

She flew off to her workshop, leaving the strange thing next to the stream.

At that moment, Beck was hurrying along the bank of Havendish Stream. She was on her way to visit a family of squirrels. Beck was so busy thinking of the games she wanted to play with her friends that she didn't see the strange object lying on the ground.

"Oh!" she cried as her foot got caught on it. She tumbled over the thing and landed beside it.

Beck looked closely at the object she had tripped over. "What's this?" she asked. Suddenly, Beck had a great idea.

She picked up the object. It was the perfect thing to bring to the squirrels!

"Look what I've brought!" Beck cried in Squirrel when she arrived at their tree. "Isn't it amazing? It's a squirrel scratcher!"

The two youngest squirrels wrestled each other for the chance to be first.

"Don't worry," Beck said, "everyone will have a turn!"

She gave one of the squirrels a little scratch behind the ears. He chittered happily.

Beck spent the rest of the morning brushing the squirrels' tails and scratching their bellies.

When it was time to go, Beck promised the squirrels that she would bring the scratcher on her next visit.

She flew back to her room. The scratcher was too big to store in there, so she left it nestled between the roots of a tall oak tree.

"It should be safe here," Beck said aloud.

Meanwhile, Tink was in her workshop trying to scrub a tall, narrow pot that she had just finished repairing.

"Hi, Tink, are you busy?" her friend Terence said, poking his head in the door.

"Come on in, Terence," Tink said grumpily.

"What's wrong?" he asked.

"It's this pot," Tink told him. "I can't reach the bottom!"

"What you need is a long-handled pot scrubber," Terence said. He quickly described a tool with a long handle and a bunch of prickly bristles at one end.

Tink blinked in astonishment. Terence had just described the lost thing she'd found that morning!

Not far away, Lily, a garden-talent fairy, was resting on a branch in a tall oak tree. She had spent the entire morning scaring shimmer beetles away from her garden. The beetles loved to eat her flowers.

As Lily set off for her garden again, she spotted an object below. She flew down to examine it. Suddenly, she had an idea!

She brought the object back to her garden and planted it near her flowers. She dressed it up to look like a fairy.

When she was done, Lily hid behind a large flower. After a few moments, a shimmer beetle flew toward the flowers. But when it saw the "fairy," it flew off.

"It works!" Lily cheered. "My scare-bug works!"

Meanwhile, Tink and Terence headed back to Havendish Stream. But the pot scrubber was nowhere to be found.

"Tink! Terence!" Beck shouted. She flew toward them.

"Beck, what's wrong?" Terence asked.

"I left my squirrel scratcher beside the tall oak tree and now it's gone!" Beck said. "Have you seen it?"

"No," Tink replied, "but my long-handled pot scrubber is gone, too!"

Beck gasped.

"It sounds like there's a thief in Pixie Hollow," Terence said.

The fairies quickly split up and went to search for the lost things.

Beck entered Lily's garden.

"Tink! Terence!" she hollered. "Over here! I found my squirrel scratcher!"

Tink flew over. "That's not a squirrel scratcher," she said. "It's a long-handled pot scrubber."

Just then, Lily flew up. "What do you think of my scare-bug?" she asked.

"Scare-bug?" Tink cried. "It's a pot scrubber!"

"No, it's a squirrel scratcher!" Beck said.

The three fairies fought back and forth with one another about what the lost object was.

Suddenly, a dark shadow fell over the garden. It was a hawk! And it was diving right for the fairies.

"Look out!" Beck shouted.

The fairies scattered around the garden. They hid inside flowers and under leaves.

The hawk swooped down and grabbed the scare-bug! It flew off with the object clasped tightly in its claws.

Tink looked around. After a few moments, she came out of her hiding place. The other fairies slowly emerged as well.

Suddenly, their argument over the lost thing seemed silly. Tink looked at her friends. She knew they felt as bad as she did.

Tink cleared her throat. "I wonder what that thing is really for," she said.

"I guess we'll never know," Beck replied.

"Maybe it's a fairy lifesaver," Lily said.

The other fairies smiled. They could certainly agree with that.

Iridessa Forgets

"Fira, is this where you're keeping the spare rainbows?" Iridessa called to the other light-talent fairy. But Fira didn't hear her. Iridessa flew a little closer. "Fira?"

Fira spun around. "Iridessa!" she exclaimed.

"I just wanted to know if this is where you're keeping the spare rainbows," Iridessa said.

"This is the place," Fira replied. She looked at the pile of rainbows. "We can never be too prepared, right? Isn't this your favorite time of year?"

"Yes, I love getting ready for spring," Iridessa said. "I have a few more things to do before dinner, though. See you later, Fira!"

As Iridessa flew away, she pulled a large leaf on which she'd written her to-do list out of her pocket. The fairies would be bringing spring to the mainland in just two days. They had a lot of work left to do.

Iridessa loved preparing for a new season. It gave her an excuse to really get organized. The first thing she always did was make a list of all the things she needed to do.

When Iridessa got to the meadow, she settled down on her favorite log and studied her list. "Give extra rainbows to Fira," she said. "Check!"

Iridessa read through her list once. Then she read through it again. She was starting to get a funny feeling.

It wasn't the happy feeling she usually got from checking things off her list. It wasn't the nervous feeling she got when there was a lot of work to do, either.

"I'm forgetting something," Iridessa said.

"What are you forgetting?" a voice said.

Iridessa leaped into the air. "Oh, Iris! I didn't see you there."

The garden-talent fairy was standing in the tall grass, holding a thick book.

"I thought I saw a rare type of clover in this meadow," Iris said. "I wanted to put it in my gardening book. But I can't seem to find the clover now."

"That's frustrating," Iridessa said. "I don't like losing things."

"Neither do I. I also don't like forgetting things," Iris said. "That's why I always write everything down in my book."

"That's why I made a list," Iridessa said. "But I still think something is missing."

"If there's anything a garden talent can do to help, let me know," Iris said before she flew off.

Iridessa didn't think Iris could help, but maybe another garden-talent fairy could. Rosetta was one of her best friends. She knew how important staying organized was to Iridessa. Maybe she could help figure out what was missing. Iridessa flew off toward Rosetta's garden.

The garden was even more beautiful than usual today. Rosetta was getting ready for spring as well, and her garden was filled with the crocuses and daffodils she planned to bring to the mainland. As Iridessa approached, she could see that Rosetta was testing a new color of paint on a sweet pea.

"Dessa, look!" Rosetta called when she saw her friend. "This pale purple color you helped me pick out is just perfect!"

Iridessa smiled. The flowers almost glowed in the late afternoon light.

"They do look great. You'll be all set to bring spring to the mainland!" Iridessa said. "But, um . . . Rosetta, I'm having a little trouble with my preparations."

Rosetta immediately put down the paint. "You?" she said. "But you're always so on top of everything."

"Well, I have my list, as always," Iridessa said, showing Rosetta the leaf. "But I have this awful feeling that I'm forgetting something."

Rosetta looked over the list with her friend. Finally, she said, "Dess, all of these are checked off. You're not forgetting anything. You're all done!"

Iridessa shook her head. "It's not the things on the list I'm worried about," she said. "I think I might have forgotten to put something on the list in the first place."

Rosetta laughed. "Dessa, since the day you arrived, you have never once left anything off your lists," she said. "You're worrying for nothing. Come on, it's almost time for dinner!"

When Iridessa and Rosetta got to the Tea Room, they saw their friends Fawn, Terence, and Silvermist sitting at their table. The serving-talent fairies were hurrying to deliver dandelion rolls to all the tables. They knew the other talents had to get back to their work.

"It must be hard making sure everyone has enough pixie dust to get to the mainland and back," Fawn was saying to Terence.

"It is a lot of work," Terence admitted. "We still have more to do."

"We do, too," the animal-talent fairy replied. She turned to Iridessa and Rosetta, who had just sat down. "How is it going for you two?"

"Dessa's all done!" Rosetta said. She picked up the teapot and began to pour a cup for herself.

"I thought I was," Iridessa said. "But I know I'm forgetting something important."

"Do you have enough sunbeams ready?" Fawn asked.

"Yes, and a whole extra batch just in case. Moonbeams, too," Iridessa replied.

Silvermist placed her hand on Iridessa's shoulder. "I know you're worried," she said, "but I'm sure you haven't forgotten anything. You're Iridessa! You don't forget!"

It did make Iridessa feel a little better to know that her friends trusted her so much. She smiled as she flew away from the Tea Room. Perhaps they were right. Maybe she was already prepared for spring and didn't need to worry.

"Tinker Bell! Cheese is ready!" a fairy called out.

Iridessa twirled around and saw an animal-talent fairy hooking up Tink's mouse friend to a cart full of pixie dust.

Tink is great at solving problems. Maybe she can help me think of what I'm forgetting, thought Iridessa.

Iridessa flew toward the cart. The pixie dust made her wings tingle with magic. "Tink," she said, "why are you hauling dust?"

"Iridessa! Do you want to ride with me? This cart broke a wheel, and I told Terence I'd fix it," Tink said, hitting the wheel with her hammer. "Now I've got to get it back to him fast."

Iridessa nodded and climbed onto the cart next to her friend.

The light talent looked around as Cheese pulled them through Pixie Hollow. Dozens of fairies flew past, hurrying to get their work done in time.

"It's starting to get dark," Iridessa said. "Almost time for the—"

Just then, a swarm of fireflies swept out from behind a tree and hovered over the fairies. Their light helped the fairies work long after the sun had set.

"Oh!" Iridessa gasped.

Tink looked around. "You and the other light talents always do such a nice job lighting the fireflies," she said. Then she noticed the look on her friend's face. "What's wrong, Dess?"

"The fireflies!" Iridessa pulled out her list again. Every item had been checked off. But tomorrow, the last day of preparation, was Iridessa's day to provide light to work by. Most of the fairies would be working late into the night to finish everything. The fireflies wouldn't be able to help them. They'd be resting before their trip to the mainland the next day.

"Oh, no, Tink!" Iridessa cried. "The fireflies can't work tomorrow night and go to the mainland for spring the next day!"

"What do you mean?" Tinker Bell asked. "Why can't they do both?"

"Tomorrow is the busiest night of the year!" Iridessa said. "If the fireflies have to light Pixie Hollow, they'll be too tired to go to the mainland for spring! Spring wouldn't be the same without fireflies!"

Tinker Bell tugged on her bangs. "But there won't be any spring at all if there isn't any light in Pixie Hollow tomorrow night," she said. "The fairies still have a lot of work to do!"

Iridessa knew Tink was right. She looked down at her list. But it couldn't help her anymore. "Tink," she said, "I have to go."

Iridessa hurried to find
Fira. As she approached, she
could see Fira surrounded
not only by rainbows, but by
huge piles of sunbeams and
moonbeams as well. The light
talents had worked so hard to
get ready. And now, because

of Iridessa, they wouldn't have everything done in time after all.

"Iridessa! Look at all our supplies!" Fira said when she saw her
friend. "We have twice as much as we need."

"Actually, we don't." Iridessa's lower lip trembled. "It's all my
fault," she said. "I forgot to plan ahead for lighting Pixie Hollow
tomorrow night."

Fira smiled. She held out her arms toward the enormous pile of
sunbeams. "Everything is going to be fine."

The next evening, Iridessa held a cup of sunbeams over Tinker Bell's shoulder while she fixed a cracked flowerpot.

"That's perfect, Dessa!" Tink said. "How lucky that you had already collected so many sunbeams. This is even better than having the fireflies around. Where are they, anyway?"

"They're resting for tomorrow's journey," Iridessa replied. She smiled and held the light higher. Now she knew what it felt like to be a firefly. It was a moment she would never forget.

The Perfect Painting

Bess whistled as she flew through the woods. The art-talent fairy was on her way to her studio. She couldn't wait to get started on a new painting.

"Where are you off to in such a hurry?" a voice called.

Bess paused in midair. Then she saw her friend Fira resting on a flower patch.

"To my studio!" Bess said. "I want to make the perfect painting to hang on the wall. Something that will inspire me every time I look at it."

"Good luck!" Fira replied. She waved as Bess zipped away.

"Where is Bess going?" someone asked.

Fira turned around and saw Rani walking toward her. "Bess is off to her studio," Fira said. "She needs some inspiration."

Rani gasped. "Bess isn't feeling inspired?"

"She is, but—" Fira began to explain.

But Rani wasn't listening. "I know just what she needs!" she said and hurried off.

Rani skipped along a path through the meadow. By the time she arrived at Havendish Stream, she was bursting with excitement.

As a water-talent fairy, Rani was always happiest when she was close to water. She knelt beside the stream and peered into it.

After a moment, Rani plucked a smooth stone from the water. "It's perfect!" she cried.

"What's perfect?" Tinker Bell asked, flying up behind her.

Rani grinned at her friend. "This!" she exclaimed, holding out the stone. "Fira says Bess needs some inspiration," Rani told Tink. "And I thought, what's more inspiring than a beautiful stone that has been worn smooth by the water? I can't wait for Bess to see it!" Rani said and skipped off.

"Inspiration?" Tink said to herself. Whenever she needed inspiration, she looked at a small silver bowl in her workshop. It had been her first repair as a tinker fairy in Never Land.

"That's it!" Tink cried. "I know just what Bess needs."

Moments later, Tinker Bell was on her way to Bess's studio. She was struggling to carry a large copper pot.

"Let me help you, Tink," her friend Lily, a garden talent, called. "Where are you taking that pot?"

Tink told the garden talent that she was bringing the pot to Bess for inspiration.

"My violets are very inspiring!" Lily exclaimed. "We can plant one of them in this pot."

The two fairies flew to Lily's garden. Lily chose her most beautiful flower and arranged it in the pot.

"Perfect!" Lily cried.

As Tink and Lily flew through the forest with the flowerpot, they spotted their friend Beck. The animal talent was sitting on a tree branch with a squirrel.

"Where are you going?" Beck called.

"To Bess's studio," Lily replied.

"Bess needs some inspiration right away!" Tink said.

"Did you hear that?" Beck asked the squirrel. "Bess is feeling uninspired."

The squirrel chattered and twitched his fluffy tail.

"Hmm," Beck replied. "I'm not saying a walnut isn't inspiring, but I have something else in mind."

Meanwhile, Bess finally arrived in the deepest part of the woods. Her art studio came into view and she smiled.

Bess's studio was a plain wooden crate

that had once been used to hold tangerines. She had found it washed up on the shore of Never Land and had used magic to move it to a very quiet, peaceful part of the woods.

"There will be no interruptions here," Bess said as she flew into the studio. "I can paint in peace all day."

Bess sat down on her stool and stared at the white birch-bark paper. She held up her paintbrush and got ready to make the first stroke . . . but she couldn't decide what to paint!

"That's odd," Bess said to herself. Usually, she was overflowing with ideas for beautiful paintings. But today her mind was blank.

"Should I paint a flower?" she asked herself. "Or a tree? Or maybe a sunset?" All of those things sounded pretty, but none of them seemed quite right.

Bess sighed and frowned at her easel. She hovered upside down, hoping that would give her an idea. But it just made her dizzy.

"Why don't I feel inspired?" Bess said as she righted herself.

Above her, the leaves rustled in the breeze. The art talent scowled up at them. "Shh!" she whispered. "I need peace and quiet to concentrate."

A bird chirped from a nearby branch. That gave Bess an idea. "Maybe if I sing something," she mused. She launched into the first verse of her favorite song, but her voice soon trailed off. She felt very silly singing to an easel.

Bess tried meditating, yelling, reciting fairy history, covering her eyes with a fern, counting to one hundred, and pretending not to care. Nothing worked.

"Oh!" Bess cried. "Why can't I think of anything?"

Finally, Bess fell flat on her back. She stared up at the ceiling.

"I'm not going to move until I get an idea for the perfect painting," she said firmly. "I mean it. I don't care if it takes the whole afternoon."

"Knock, knock!"

Bess turned and saw Fira approaching the studio.

"I wanted to see how your painting was going," Fira said. She peered strangely at Bess. "Why are you lying on the floor?"

"I was just thinking about what to paint," Bess said, climbing to her feet and dusting herself off.

"You haven't started yet?" Fira asked. "What happened?"

"Well . . ." Bess said, feeling embarrassed.

"Bess!" Tink called out. She and Lily flew toward the studio with their flowerpot. "We brought you some inspiration!"

"Me too!" Rani cried. She stepped into the clearing, followed by Beck.

Bess looked at her friends and their gifts. Tink's copper pot was so shiny, and Lily's violet was the prettiest purple she'd ever seen. The river stone Rani held was as smooth and blue as the water in Havendish Stream. Beck had brought two halves of a speckled egg, which would be great for mixing paint in. Her friends were so thoughtful.

"That's it!" Bess cried.

Bess grabbed her largest brush and darted to the longest wall in her studio. She painted as fast as she could. The other fairies watched quietly while she worked.

Finally, Bess stood back to admire her painting. She had created a picture of her friends. She smiled as she turned to look at them.

"What do you think?" Bess asked.

"It's beautiful," Lily said with a happy sigh.

"I wanted to paint the perfect picture to inspire me while I work every day," Bess said. "And as soon as you all showed up, I realized that—"

"Nothing is more inspiring than good friends!" Rani exclaimed.